THE REAL *HOODWIVES* OF DETROIT 3

A Novel By

INDIA

XOXO
India

GRADE A PUBLICATIONS
P.O. BOX 18175
FAIRFIELD, OHIO 45018

ISBN:978-0-9852280-3-3

For information regarding special discounts on bulk purchases, please contact Gradeapub@gmail.com

Manufactured in the United States of America

Cover design: Dynasty Covers Me
Editor: Cassandra Williams

FOR BOOKINGS OR SPECIAL EVENTS
CONTACT INDIA
P.O. BOX 18175
FAIRFIELD, OHIO 45018
GRADEAPUB@GMAIL.COM

Books by India

Dope, Death, and Deception

Still Deceiving

The Real Hoodwives of Detroit 1 & 2

Money Over Everything

When a Woman's Fed Up 1 & 2

(Anthology with LaShonda DeVaughn & Tracee Boyd)

Gangstress 1 & 2

This book is dedicated to
Everybody with a dream…

"Shoot for the moon. Even if you miss, you'll land among the stars."

~Brian Littrell

Acknowledgments

Glory be to God! I can't believe this is my eighth novel since 2011. It's been a long road, but I'm thankful! I've had plenty of sleepless nights, but I'm grateful! I've also endured a few bumps and bruises along the way, but I'm still here! The passion I have for writing is what keeps me in the game. So many times, I've wanted to walk away and take a break, but I can't; it's my calling. Many of you will never know or fully understand the blood, sweat, and tears I pen each creation with. However, it's always with you in mind that I challenge myself to be better, stronger, and come harder with each novel.

As my family, friends, and loyal readers, you're worth consistent quality. Therefore, I strive to serve it proper on a silver platter because you deserve the best. Most of you have had my back from day one and I'll be forever indebted to you. Your unyielding support has been amazing; I just can't thank you enough! One day, "India" will be a household name and it's because of people like: Michael,

A'yanna, Brenda, Lacy, Jason, La'mari, Cassandra, Michael Sr., Bunny, Jesse, Tonya, Terrance, Tia, Darielle, Lil' Doe, Dejaun, JDee, Luxury Mar, Erica, Audrey, Annette, Destiny, Tanya, Ms. Terry, Motorcity Moe, Mari, Toya, Taie, Valencia, Margo, Kelly, Jewels, Sheryl, Vivian, Erin, Dee, Aleta Williams, Anjela, Liz, Kathleen, Tiffany, Nosha, Gabrielle, Queen B.G., Ava, MizzLadii Redd, Rhonda, Mary, Karla, Krystál, Tiffany, Kris, Shawn, Vadie, Ericia W., Shonda DeVaughn, Tracee, Wanda, HP Drew, III, Cherch, Uncle George, Uncle Rob, the DJ Gatsby Book Club, David Weaver & the entire **TBRS family!** (The squad is way too big to name everyone).

Love, India

P.S. Spread the word about my books to your family and friends. I also encourage you to request my titles at your local libraries and bookstores. Remember, teamwork makes the dream work. Once you have read this story, please email me at: gradeapub@gmail.com or hit me up on Facebook so we can discuss your thoughts and opinions. Furthermore, I kindly ask that you provide a review on Amazon.com. Again, thank you for your support; I look forward to hearing from you.

THE REAL *HOODWIVES* OF DETROIT 3

A Novel By

INDIA

INDIA

Prologue
Chloe

As I followed behind Sam's vehicle, my thoughts went back to Lovely. I had no intentions of returning to the hospital so I pulled out the stolen cell phone and dialed the number she'd given me days ago. "Who is this?" A male's voice boomed.

"No need for names; just know that your girl has been delivered to Henry Ford Hospital. I got her out of prison. It's up to you to do the rest. You better get there fast, before she has that baby and is taken back into custody." *Click.* Silently, I prayed for my girl and hoped things worked out for her. I knew we would never see each other again but wished her well anyway.

Within half an hour, we had arrived at our destination. Sam punched in a code and entered through the gate. I parked on the street and waited ten minutes before getting out of the car. The spacing on the rod iron gate was large enough for me to squeeze through, belly and all. With every step I took toward the lavish home, I could feel the fire in my veins. I was so hot I was beginning to sweat. Creeping around to the back of the house I searched for a window or door that had been left open. *Bingo!* The kitchen window was cracked open about three inches. Calmly, I walked onto the deck then slid over a few pieces of outdoor furniture. Once the stack was tall enough for me to heist myself up into the window, I removed my shoes and stepped on. It was a little wobbly at first but it did the trick. Just like that, I was inside and one step closer to what I'd come for.

Scanning the gourmet kitchen, a butcher knife resting on the wooden cutting board caught my attention. I didn't have a gun so this would have to do. There were no lights on, which was a gift and a curse. Mina wouldn't be able to see me but it meant I wouldn't be able to see her either. "Looking for this?" WHAM, the bitch actually hit me in the back. I turned to see what her weapon of choice was then laughed when I noticed the frying pan. Thinking quickly, I dodged her next blow then sent one of my own to her thigh. The knife tore through her flesh; blood squirted everywhere. Mina was startled but unstoppable as she came at me again with the cooking utensil.

"You crazy bitch! Just leave me alone." She swung, catching me on the shoulder.

"Leave you alone!?" I looked at her sideways. "You're the one who stole my life." I tried to stab her again but she blocked me with the pan.

"It was never your life to begin with," she countered. I was tired of talking so I jabbed the knife at her face and watched the skin on her cheek separate. The face wound caused her to drop her weapon and reach for her face, giving me the advantage. I climbed on top of her with my left hand around her neck and my right hand clutching the knife. I smiled as Mina gagged and fought for air. Desperately, she tried to reach for the frying pan, which was within an inch of her grasp. "Chloe stop!" Sam's voice boomed from the entryway.

"Or what?" I rolled my eyes.

"I will kill you!" He stood trembling with a .38 in his hand. I looked down at Mina who was practically dead anyway and decided to turn my attention to Sam.

"Do it then." I walked up to him; he backed away. "You ain't shit but a pussy! Do it!" I yelled. BAM! A blow to the back of my head caused me to stumble. I tried grabbing onto the wall to hold myself up, but I slipped in Mina's blood and hit the floor.

It was unclear of how long I'd been out cold. However, I came to while being hoisted into the air on a stretcher. I looked down at my hands and ankles to see if I was cuffed, thank goodness I wasn't. An officer walked side-by-side with the medical team as they escorted me to the waiting ambulance. With only seconds to make a split decision, I grabbed the officer's gun from his holster, and shot him twice. POW! POW! Like a mad woman, I removed myself from the stretcher then surveyed the area to see what my next move would be. "Freeze! Drop the weapon!"

I turned to see three policemen with their guns raised. Come hell or high water, I wasn't going back to prison. "Drop the weapon or I will shoot!"

"Shoot me then!" I demanded. "I've seen everything except death anyway."

"Drop the weapon Chloe, please!" Sam begged. I knew his concern was more for his unborn daughter than for me, so to hell with him. Slowly, I raised the gun toward my face then opened my mouth wide. Everything moved in slow motion as I stared into his pleading eyes. He repeatedly begged me to stop, but I couldn't go back to prison, and I refused to live my life without him. I squeezed my eyes shut then pulled the trigger. BOOM!

Lovely

"Baby, I'm so glad to have you back." Maine smiled as we pulled up to the private jet awaiting our arrival behind Metro Airport. We'd been riding for almost an hour and neither of us had said a word. Instead, we chose to bask in the glory of my freedom.

"It feels good to be back." I snuggled up next to him. I knew everything would be alright from this point forward. At last, I could put this horrible situation behind me and start over. No more prison brawls or nightmares of giving up custody of my son.

"Let's go boo." He stepped from the whip then helped me out. "I'm getting you far away from here. Take one last look at Michigan because we ain't ever coming back."

"You promise?" I giggled. Something I hadn't done in months.

"I have a whole new life set up for us in Mexico," Maine beamed. Yet, at that moment, I was saddened. I didn't want a whole new life; I wanted my old life with a few alterations.

"Does that mean I have to say goodbye to Coco and Do It?" I couldn't stand the thought of living without them or my niece, Shawnie, whom I'd missed so much.

"Shawnie and Coco's boys are already down there with Agent Nichols," Maine smiled. Agent Nichols was now retired from the feds. She was sort of like the mother I'd always wanted. And I replaced the daughter she'd lost to the streets years ago.

"Are you serious?" I kissed him so hard my lips turned white. "Coco you're coming too? What about the salon?" I couldn't believe she would agree to leave her booming business behind.

"We're only coming as an extended vacation so to speak," she smiled.

"Now get your sexy self on that plane." Maine slapped my butt then turned his attention to our luggage in the trunk.

On my way to the aircraft with Coco, I paused and overheard Do It. "Yo, what you wanna do about the shorty you got in the warehouse?"

"Let the bitch post up for a few days then call her man to come get her." Maine said then proceeded to join us on the jet.

Gucci

I was filthy, hungry, and tired as all hell. Two nights inside of a condemned warehouse was starting to get the best of me. My hands were bound to a wooden board behind my back and the hay beneath my ass was extremely uncomfortable. My pants were moist from urine, and the smell was beginning to turn my stomach. The only consolation I had was the fact that, by now, Mario was combing the streets looking for me. With his pulse on the city and ear to the streets, I knew he would find me in no time. "Yo lil' mama, you hungry?" Someone asked.

"Forty-eight hours later and now you ask!" I exploded.

"Bitch, are you hungry or not?" He asked from the doorway. There were no lights on inside the warehouse. Therefore, it was impossible to see him.

"Yeah mutha fucka, I'm starving!" My stomach began to growl right at that very moment. I listened as the man walked toward me. There was something in the way he drug his foot that signified he had a previous injury to his body.

"Eat!" He threw a paper bag filled with Coney Island; I could tell by the distinct smell.

"Nigga, my hands are tied behind my back!"

This asshole wasn't working with a full deck. Reaching up, my abductor turned on the lights; I blinked rapidly.

"Gucci?" He asked with familiarity. I squinted to see who this nigga was but came up blank. "Awe shit my nigga!" He began to shake his head profusely, which caused his dreads to sway.

"I can't place you." Honestly, I didn't know this man from a can of paint.

"It's me Do It." He leaned in closer. I scanned him again and noted that without the dreads, minus a few extra pounds, and the limp, he was very familiar.

For the first time in a long time, I smiled. The man before me was my ace from way back in the day. Me, Mario, Do It, and his girlfriend, White Girl used to roll in the streets hot and heavy.

"DeShawn, man you gotta get me outta here!" I wasted no time.

"Damn G! I didn't know Maine was coming after you. I thought he was going after the other chick Mario was fucking with." Do it admitted.

"Well, I guess that plan went sideways."

"Gucci, you're my nigga from the bottom to the top. I swear I didn't know you were back here." He looked apologetic while untying me.

"So you into fuckin' kidnapping now?" If I

would've had an ounce of strength, I would've beaten his ass just off general principle.

"Chill out!" He extended a hand to pull me up. We did what was necessary to get my sister home."

"Yeah whatever!" I retorted, although I would've done the same for one of my people.

"Do you need me to call anybody for you?"

"Yeah, call my husband. I need to check on my daughter." After a few calls went unanswered, I called Claudia who informed me Maria was good. She asked me to meet her at the hospital where Mario still was.

I called Cartier; he picked me up within fifteen minutes. "You good ma?" He was concerned.

"Do I look good!?" I snapped.

"Where you want me to take you shorty?" He didn't pay my temper tantrum any mind.

"Take me to the hospital. I have a few choice words for that husband of mine." I folded my arms.

"Gucci, I know you didn't call me to pick you up and take you to see another nigga. If that's the case, you can get out now." He stopped the car in the middle of the road then lit a blunt.

"It ain't like that. I need to tell him I'm leaving."

Cartier stared at me in disbelief while blowing smoke in my direction. "You sure about that?"

"Take me to the fucking hospital!" I was in no mood to debate. Either he would drive me or I would walk.

Thirty minutes later, we pulled up to the hospital. I begged him to let me handle this on my own. I was sure it would get ugly and I didn't need that firecracker to make things worst. "Gucci, we were worried sick about you!" Mina ran up and hugged me for dear life. "Sam has been out there looking for you like crazy."

"That's funny," I smirked. "While Sam was combing the streets, where was my bitch ass husband? Let me guess…laid up with his trick?"

"Gucci, I think you should talk to Mario." She looked sad.

"That's exactly what I plan to do." I laughed sarcastically then barged into his room, prepared to put everybody out.

Nikki

As we all stood silently surrounding Mario's hospital bed, Gucci burst into the room with an attitude, demanding that everybody leave. "I'm so glad you're okay G." Mario spoke softly.

"No thanks to you bastard!" She yelled. "You left me out there to die."

"G..." Mario tried to talk but she cut him off.

"Fuck you and that funky bitch! If you want her, you can have her because I've moved on." She removed her oversized wedding ring then tossed it to the ground. I had to laugh when she called me funky because her ass was the one smelling like piss and serious body odor.

"Gucci, please stop yelling." Mario tried calming her down.

"Nigga, you ain't heard yelling yet!" She yelled even louder than before.

"Gotdammit shut the fuck up! I don't need to have this shit on my mind before I go under the knife!" Rio yelled then immediately grabbed his head. Gucci stood there looking dumbfounded.

Under the advice of the doctors, Rio had decided to have the surgery. He tried to wait for Sam to find Gucci. Unfortunately, every day the bullet stayed lodged in his brain it swelled up and would eventually prove to be deadly. This morning he requested I be present with Junior. Ms. C was there with Maria. Sam had even shown up with Mina. It was a rainy day and for some reason my stomach was in knots. I didn't know if we were saying goodbye or see ya later. Nevertheless, it was all too much for me. The only sound in the room was that of the children. Maria giggled as Junior made silly faces at her. They didn't understand the severity of the situation. I prayed their father returned safely from surgery so they would never have to.

After an awkward silence, Mario spoke up. "Feels good to see my family together again."

"I know it does son." Ms. C rubbed his free hand since the other one was covered with an I.V. tube. No one else uttered a sound; we simply hung onto Mario's every word.

"I wanted everyone here today so I could get a few things straight," he began. "First off, Sam I'm glad you came back."

"Glad to be back bro." Sam replied.

"I know you're done with the street life but if anything happens to me please make sure H.O.F. lives forever. You don't have to run it yourself, just find a good replacement for me. A lot of people eat off the money H.O.F. brings in. It's important for me to keep it that way. Can you do that?" Mario asked.

"Ain't nothing gon' happen to you man." Sam waved Mario off.

"I might not come back out here the way I'm going in. I need to know you can handle what I'm asking?" Mario asked in a firm tone.

"I got you, fa sho!" Sam appeared sad but held his emotions in check.

"Mina, you better keep my boy happy you hear me. Sometimes in life you don't get second chances. Now that you have one, you better run with that shit," Mario laughed.

"I'm running down the altar with my second chance." She flashed a rock and I smiled.

"Mama I..." Unexpectedly, Rio got choked up, which caused me to tear up.

"Yes son?"

"Mama, I love you and I'm sorry." He broke down like a baby.

"Sorry for what son?" Claudia blew her nose.

"I should've chosen a different path for my life. You always said if I live by the streets, I would die by the streets. I should've listened," Mario sniffed. I resisted the urge to wipe the tears rolling down his face.

Ms. C couldn't take anymore. She broke down

crying then ran into the private bathroom. Mario looked at Gucci and began again. "G, you're my best friend and that shit will never change. You've done more dirt with and for me than ten niggas put together. The bond we have is irreplaceable, our daughter is proof of that." I looked at Gucci who was on the verge of passing out. I knew the pain of this situation was just as hurtful for her as it was for me. She needed someone to lean on. I did too, so I take hold of her hand and held it as tight as I could. I love you Gucci but I'm not in love with you. No matter how much we both tried it just wasn't meant to be." Rio continued. "My heart belongs to Nikki and it always will. Maybe in the next lifetime, there will be another time and another place for you and me," he sniffed. "I heard most gangstas go to heaven; so I'll hold you a spot. In the meantime, tell Cartier to treat you right." Mario sniffed again.

"Why are talking like you're about to die?" Gucci screamed but Mario didn't respond.

"Nikki." At the sound of my name, my knees buckled. "I love you like a fat kid love cake girl," he laughed. "I'm sorry I fucked this up for us baby. If I could do this shit differently, I would. If by some miracle I walk out of this shit alive, I want you to be my wife again. I want to start over far away from here with our new bundle of joy." On that note, everyone looked my way except for Gucci, who was still holding my hand. I sobbed because he truly loved me unconditionally. "Nik, I love you more than life itself. Anything that is a part of you is a part of me, no matter what." He smiled while I continued sobbing.

Just then, the doctor came to roll Mario out for surgery. "Look, if I don't make it, just promise to keep my family together." Finally, he released the water works. "Y'all squash the beef so my kids can grow up together. Keep them as far away from street life as possible so they'll have a chance to be something in life."

"I love you Rio." I called out, running up to give him a kiss.

"Aye, if shit go sideways in there, tell my new baby his father died a gangsta nothing more, nothing less." He rubbed my belly and winked as the hospital staff rolled him away.

INDIA

One Week Later

Chapter One

Nikki

It was a somber day in the city of Detroit. The clouds hung low and rain was in the forecast. From my bedroom window, I could see the trees swaying from side-to-side, a telltale sign that a storm was brewing. "You look pretty mommy." Junior lay on my bed playing with toy cars. He looked handsome in the black slacks, white t-shirt, and navy blue, Ralph Lauren sweater vest.

"Thank you little man." I flashed him a half-hearted smile and continued to get dressed. The black spandex dress fit every curve of my size ten body. My small pregnant belly was barely noticeable. The black hat and funeral veil may have been a tad bit much. However, something was needed to cover the bags beneath my eyes. I'd been crying nonstop; my face was a swollen mess. Typically, I would've chosen sunglasses. They weren't appropriate for such a sad occasion. The mere thought of the funeral I was preparing to attend had me in tears, yet again. I grabbed a Kleenex from the box on the dresser. Death is never easy to deal with, especially when you lose someone close to your heart.

"Why are you crying mommy?" Junior was concerned, but I had to be strong and put on a brave facade. He didn't need to be burdened with my sorrows.

"I had something in my eye but I'm okay now."

"Are you sure?" His voice was squeaky and baby-like.

"I'm sure." After reassuring him, I slipped into the black, slingback pumps, and watched my phone dance across the dresser. It was vibrating. "Hello."

"Hey cuz, how are you holding up?" My cousin, Anjela asked with genuine concern. Shrugging my shoulders as if she could see me, I replied, "I'm good, I guess."

"That's good," she sighed. "I really wish I could've been there for you today but duty calls." She had been hired by the disgruntled husband of a reality star in Los Angeles. He wanted to sue his wife for deformation of character and custody of their children. Anjela met the man at a charity event; he hired her shortly thereafter. "Anyway, I was calling you on my way to the airport to let you know I love you and I'll be back in a few days."

"Thanks cuz. Have a safe trip." I ended the call then placed my phone into the purse on the nightstand. "Ready little man?"

"Are we going to go play with daddy?" His eyes were wide with anticipation.

"No baby, not today."

"Where are we going mommy?"

"We're going to a funeral." I knew this would start the game of twenty-questions.

"What's a funeral?"

"A funeral is a celebration for someone who has passed away Junior." I helped him down from the bed, grabbed my purse, and headed down the stairs to the SUV.

"Who passed away mommy?" He was such an inquisitive kid. Before I could part my lips to respond, my phone started vibrating again. *Thank God for perfect timing!*

"Hey Rio."

"What's up Nik; what time are you coming up here?" He was so spoiled it was ridiculous. It was only ten o'clock in the morning and he was already calling to see where I was.

His surgery last week was a success. Doctors removed the bullet from his skull. Now, he's as good as new! They were keeping him for observation though. Miraculously, he was only left with a visible scar on the right side of his head, which is about three inches long. Mario was pissed that he had to cut his long, curly, jet black hair. It was his signature look. As quiet as it's kept, I actually like the low-cut Caesar and deep waves better. It gave him a mature, age appropriate vibe. "Hello! Did you hear me?"

"My bad, I was strapping Junior into the car seat." I closed the backdoor then got into the driver's seat. "I might not make it there today."

"Why not?" Just like a child, he pouted.

"Today is Chloe's funeral. Remember I told you she tried to kill herself with the police officer's gun."

"That rat should've fucking died as a mouse!" Mario scoffed. His disdain for my friend was no shocker. However, it was very disrespectful being that she was deceased.

"Rio, that's no way to talk about dead people!"

"I can't believe you going to that bullshit anyway!" He was on ten right about now.

"She was my friend."

"She was a snitch!" He barked. "Fuck outta here with that my friend shit! Homegirl was a liar, a con artist, and a cop!"

"Everything you said is true. Yet again, she was my friend." I've cried with that girl, partied with her, and we've seen each other through the good and bad times of the game. Mario could think whatever he wanted to think, but Chloe was like my little sister. Yeah, she was on some grimey shit. Still, all-in-all, she was good people. She didn't deserve to die at six months pregnant, even if it was her that pulled the trigger. Her daughter was in the hospital fighting for her life; and her mother had never laid eyes on her.

Sam called me on the night of the incident and told me to meet him and Mina at Children's Hospital. He explained that Chloe had taken a shot to the face. It caused internal bleeding, which filled her lungs basically suffocating her. During the process of being rushed to the hospital, she died. In fear of losing the baby, they transported Chloe's body to Children's Hospital where doctors surgically removed little Chloe from her mother's womb. I was heartbroken about the whole situation; the loss of a friend, the sadness of Sam, and the fact that their daughter would never know her mother.

"Nik, you there?"

"I'm here but let me call you back later alright." I didn't even wait for a response as I ended the call and proceeded to the funeral home.

INDIA

Chapter Two
Gucci

"I'ma be fresh as hell if the feds watching...I'ma be fresh as hell if the feds watching." I looked at the caller ID on my cell phone before answering. "What up doe?"

"Gucci are you okay? Girl, I've been worried sick about you. You haven't been returning my calls or text messages." Mina sounded displeased with me, yet relieved that I was ok.

"My bad girl; I've just been going through it that's all," I sighed. Ever since Mario's surgery, I've been missing in action. Part of me didn't want to know the outcome, be it good or bad. My heart couldn't take news of his demise. On the other hand, I didn't wanna find out he made it through surgery and crawled his ass back to Nikki. Either way, Mario would no longer belong to me.

"I understand; but you had me ready to come over there and bust your door down. Don't ever play me like that," she scolded.

"I'm sorry; it won't happen again. I'm just angry." I didn't want to admit the truth but it was time to be set free. Never in a million years could I fathom losing Mario twice in one lifetime to the same bitch. All of the rage and jealousy I felt during my teenage years was back. I still remember the day he brought that syditty bitch around. I didn't like her then, I don't like her now. There was just something about Nikki that irritated the fuck out of me. I realize we consoled one another at the hospital. However, that was under extenuating circumstances. If I saw that bitch right now, I would spit in her face.

"Are you still there?" Mina broke me free of the trancelike state I was in.

"Yeah, what were you saying?" She had been talking for over five minutes and I hadn't heard one word.

"I said Mario pulled through the surgery and is just fine." Her words were both a gift and a curse.

"Good." I was relieved, yet reluctant because I didn't know where our relationship stood.

"Well, I just wanted to let you know in case you were wondering. I'll call you when I leave Chloe's funeral."

"Why are you going to her funeral?"

"I'm going because it's the right thing to do." Mina was always being a Good Samaritan.

"Bullshit!" It was no secret that I despised Chloe while she was living. Therefore, I damn sure wouldn't be fake about it now. The rat bitch could rest in hell for eternity in my opinion.

"You're a mess," she laughed. "I'll call you later." She ended the call. I placed my phone down on the nightstand just in time for the doorbell. It was Satin. She was coming over today to watch Maria while I went to handle some business.

Today was the second day of the month, in all the hoods across America that meant payday. Every government funded dopefiend depended on social security checks to feed their habits. Those checks came on the first and fifteenth of the month. Therefore, on the second and sixteenth of each month, we collected all the earnings that were received at our spots the previous nights. Mario may have been in the hospital, but I was still about getting my bread. Having him out of the picture meant more moolah for me.

As I pulled the whip up to the grey and black house on Griggs, I put on my game face before stepping onto the gravel in my Prada sneakers. From the expressions on everyone's face outside, I could tell no one was expecting me. "What the fuck is all this?" I shouted after emerging from the car. No one said anything so I continued. "This ain't no mutha fuckin' hangout spot!" There was one nigga standing on the porch, two niggas conversing on the sidewalk, and four niggas playing dice on the side of the house.

"Chill lil' mama. My man and them only came through to smoke a blunt with me. As soon as we put it out, they're leaving." The youngin' on the front porch had the nerve to speak to me like I was tripin'.

"Lil' nigga, don't ever in your life tell me to chill!" I stepped up between his legs. "You and your mans and them can get the fuck on. Go smoke a blunt at your mama's house. I pay your young ass to work not kick it with your friends."

"Yo bro, tell ole girl to calm down." He looked pass me, addressing Neo, who was the head of this trap. Neo said nothing; he recognized the youngin' had fucked up. With a huge smile on his face, he simply shook his head.

Obviously, the newcomer had no idea who I was. It was time to introduce myself. WHACK. I backhanded the shit out of his pathetic face and watched blood squirt from his lip. Carefully, I inspected my diamond to make sure it was still intact. "What the fuck!" He jumped up ready to box but eyed Neo for approval.

"Don't look at him; look at me! I'm the boss." I yelled for every dude on the block to hear. "Did you know that?"

"I thought Mario ran the H.O.F. organization."

He said in a defiant tone. "Ain't you just his side piece?"

There were several pairs of eyes that bucked at the brash remark, including mine. This youngster was trying me; it was time to make an example outta his ass. "Side piece! Did you just call me a fuckin' side piece?" I smirked. "Take this little nigga to the basement." I demanded in a cold voice. Neo did as instructed. "Everybody else needs to clear out." After dismissing the gang of young boys outside, I proceeded through the front door of the three bedroom home. It was a typical trap house, nothing special. There was plastic up to all the windows, a dopefiend nodding on one of the folding chairs, and there was a girl at the kitchen stove whipping up work. In most traps, the women were always butt naked, but this girl was fully dressed in a halter top, spandex jeans, and a pair of four inch heels. "Hey Layna." She was Neo's main girl and the mother of his twin boys. They had both worked for us for approximately three years; I thought she was cool.

"What's up G?" She looked up briefly then went back to cooking the crack. "I told that little nigga to be easy but he's hardheaded."

"Well his ass is gon' learn today." As I proceeded toward the basement, I heard a baby crying. Stopping dead in my tracks, with a frown, I turned on the heels of my feet. "Layna, I know that ain't what I think it is." If this girl had her kids up in the trap, I was gonna whoop her ass too.

"No, it's not one of my boys, but Diesel did bring some crackhead and her baby over here last night." Again, she never removed her eyes from the boiling pot. Layna was a pro at whipping up work. "They're in the back."

"What the fuck is this, the Motel 6 or something?" Deciding to put my business in the basement on hold, I headed in the direction of the bedroom where the sound was coming from.

Pushing the door open, I never expected to find a small child standing in the middle of the floor crying while her mom had a train ran on her. The young girl who looked to be no older than seventeen was down on her knees butt naked. I watched as Diesel slammed into her ass wildly and another nigga palmed the back of her head while she sucked and gagged. Her eyes were closed. It was evident she wasn't enjoying the party. "Stop this shit now!" I demanded.

"Naw bitch, you gon' let me bust all in that first." Diesel didn't even know it was me who made the announcement.

"It's Gucci and I said stop!"

"My…my bad boss lady." He stuttered yet still pumped, trying hard to keep the rhythm.

"If you don't stop right now, I will blow your balls off!" The mention of his balls being in jeopardy halted him immediately. The other man reluctantly pulled his joint from old girl's mouth and zipped his jeans up.

"Alright boss lady, my bad!" Diesel raised his hand in surrender.

"Sweetheart, how old are you?" I tossed the girl her clothes from the floor.

"I'm twenty," she lied.

"Do you even know where you are or what you're doing?"

"Yes." She admitted shamefully.

"This is no place for you let alone your daughter." I wanted to remove my belt and beat her ass, but I wasn't her mother. "Do you have somewhere you can go?"

"Yes ma'am." She was now fully dressed in a dingy, yellow top and dirty, white bottoms. Her gym shoes had seen better days. I felt bad for the young mother. Sadly, this was life in the trap. Over the years, I'd witnessed some incredibly upsetting events. After awhile, you become immune.

Once the girl, her kid, and the other nigga were out of the room, I scolded Diesel. "What in the fuck is wrong with you? First of all, your thirty-four year old ass has no business messing with that baby. Secondly, your pedophile ass should've known better than to bring her here. And third, since when did you start fucking crackheads?"

"Gucci, it ain't even like that." He rubbed his bald head.

"So what is it like then?" I crossed my arms, awaiting his answer.

"She came over yesterday, got two rocks, and told me she would be back after she cashed her check. When she didn't come back, I went looking for her. When I found her, she still didn't have any money. So I had to teach shorty a lesson."

"Negro, you sound stupid!" I smacked my lips. "Do you know what happens when you fuck crackheads?"

"I know G." He put his head down.

"Diesel, I ain't your mama; and I can't tell you what to do with your dick. However, I will put a bullet in your ass if I catch you doing that shit in my spot again." I left him standing there then headed back toward the basement.

Upon entering the mid-size room with wooden wall panels and tiled floors, I glanced down at my watch. These niggas and their shenanigans had me late for my next pick up. The youngster was standing against the wall with a scowl. Neo was sitting on a folding chair texting. "What are you frowned up for? I'm the one who should be pissed off!"

"I ain't even do nothing." He began pleading his case.

"What's your name?" Since Neo was the one in charge of this location, I left all the hiring up to him. Many runners and corner boys came through here looking for work. I didn't have time to get to know each individual.

"Antoine."

"How much money do you make working here Antoine?"

"'Bout two hundred dollars a day." He did a quick calculation in his head.

"So that's around fourteen hundred dollars a week right?"

"Yeah, I guess," he shrugged.

"Can you make that kind of money at McDonalds or Burger King?"

"The hell if I know!" His smart mouth was gonna be the death of him. WHACK! I backhanded him again and again until his face was a bloody mess. If he wasn't a kid, I would've done more damage than that. Had he been a few years older, his ass may not have lived to see tomorrow.

"Tell you what little nigga." I paused to catch my breath. "You go and work for one of them mutha fuckas then come back and let me know."

"This is some bullshit!" He spoke under his breath while heading toward the basement stairs. "Neo, it's like that?" He turned around, hoping Neo would overturn my decision.

"She's the boss. You need to learn to be more appreciative. Gucci got more stripes out on these streets than most niggas you know. On your way to Burger King, stop somebody and ask about her." Neo and I cracked up laughing.

When the little boy was out of sight, it was time to scold Neo. "You know the way you running this bitch is all wrong, right?" I looked him square in the face. "You got niggas all outside. You got young bitches and babies in the backroom. Man, you blowing up the spot."

"My fault boss. Today was just a bad day is all," he sighed. "It won't happen again.

"Better not or you'll be headed to Burger King too.

Chapter Three
Mina

"Are you sure you don't wanna come in?" I asked Sam from the parking lot of the funeral home on W. Grand Boulevard. Although it wasn't the ideal spot to say goodbye to a loved one, it was all we could afford. Since Chloe had no family, Sam and I decided to foot the bill. It's no secret that I wasn't fond of her. Nevertheless, the situation really tugged on my heart strings. I had never seen death so close; it shook me to the core.

"No, I'm going to the hospital to be with my daughter." He was dead set against paying his final respects to his baby's mama.

"Suit yourself, just be back in about an hour." I stepped from the car and closed the door behind me. Sam waited until I was inside before he pulled off.

The place was small and quiet. The only sound I heard was a recording of someone playing the organ. "May I help you?" An elderly woman dressed in a black pantsuit smiled. She looked like she was close to death herself. The wig she wore was outdated, her makeup was overdone, and her dentures were about a size too big.

"Yes ma'am. I'm here for the service of Robyn."

I couldn't think of her last name right away but the woman knew who I was referring to.

"Right this way." She escorted me toward a room that was down the hall on the right-hand side.

Upon entrance into the small room, I was startled at the emptiness. I knew she didn't have any family. However, I did expect to see a few co-workers or friends. Beside myself, there was only Nikki and her son. I didn't know what to do. Therefore, I approached the casket then stared down at the woman who had tried to kill me. She looked good if that was a compliment. The funeral makeup was done perfectly. Her hair was styled in a simple wrap and the yellow skirt suit was nice. I picked it up from Burlington Coat Factory along with the costume jewelry she wore. "Rest in peace Chloe," I patted her hand then headed toward Nikki.

"Hi Mina," she sniffed. There was a tissue box on her lap and her nose was running.

"Hey Nikki. How are you holding up?" I took the seat next to her, sitting my purse between us. She and I weren't friends; I doubted we would ever be. In spite of this, we always remained cordial whenever in one another's presence. Now that Sam was back hanging with Mario, we would be seeing a lot of each other. Gucci wouldn't like it but I had no choice.

"I'm good. I just can't believe she's gone ya know." She blew her nose.

"Yeah, it's sad how it ended, but she's in a better place now." Although I could've, I steered clear of speaking negatively. Chloe wasn't right in the head. I didn't want to ruin Nikki's memories of who she thought her friend was. "I can't believe we're the only ones here."

"I know right." Nikki looked around the room as if something had changed. "Maybe nobody knows."

"They ran the story in the paper," I informed her. "Maybe her street friends didn't want to come for fear of her police friends being here."

"I guess," Nikki shrugged. "How are Sam and the baby?" She hadn't been to the hospital since the baby was born.

"Sam is okay. As a matter of fact, he just went to the hospital to check on Samantha." Sam had decided to name his daughter after him. He was a proud dad and I was a proud stepmom. For now, we had to pray that she pulled through the next month or so. She was so tiny she could fit in the palm of your hand. Her little body was in an incubator, and she was connected to several different machines. Even so, we were confident she would be fine and couldn't wait to bring her home.

"I'm glad to hear that. I can't wait to visit her again." Nikki shifted Junior, who was asleep across her lap. "I've just been so busy with Rio."

"I heard he pulled through the surgery and is almost as good as new." Since the doctors had wheeled him into surgery, I hadn't been back to visit him at the hospital. Things were very awkward now that he and Gucci were on the outs. Although Sam had visited several times, I was Gucci's friend and more concerned with her well-being.

"Yeah, he's back to getting on my nerves." She laughed and so did I. Just then, there was a creaking sound coming from the door behind us, causing both Nikki and I to turn. I didn't recognize the chocolate stranger being followed by three kids. Whoever it was had Nikki looking all crazy. "Roscoe is that you?" She squinted.

"What's up Nik?" He nodded with watery eyes. Before he could utter another word, she was up on her feet, and in his face.

"I thought you were dead!"

"It's a long story; I promise to explain everything. First, please let me and my kids say goodbye to my sister." He stepped pass Nikki and went over to the black casket where Chloe lay peacefully.

"Your sister?" Nikki and I both asked at the same time. From what I knew, Chloe had no family.

"Just give me a second alright!" He snapped.

"Oh I'll give you a second before I'm on the phone with Mario. Actually, I think I'll let him get to the bottom of this." She retrieved her phone then proceeded to dial. Before she could punch in the sixth number, he was pulling her toward the back of the room.

INDIA

Chapter Four
Lovely

Death is a loss that leaves you feeling empty, a feeling that I've experienced over and over throughout the years. My heart was heavy with grief and my head hung low with depression. Life had taken its toll on me; I couldn't take anymore. *I wonder what it would be like to end it all right here, right now.* I questioned myself. There was a nine millimeter handgun resting under my pillow. It was locked and loaded. All I had to do was grab it and pull the trigger. The mere thought of leaving Maine saddened me. At least, I could be with my family again. Shit didn't work out for us on earth. Perhaps Heaven held a new fate for my loved ones. I've longed for the days to see my mother and father united and happy. I've missed laughing with my big and little sisters. I wanted to see my son again and nurture him like a mother should. Instead, I was robbed of motherhood. Like a thief in the night, my son was taken from me. *That's it!* I wiped away the tears falling from my eyes then grabbed the gun.

"Lo, are you alright?" Do It stepped into the dark room without knocking, limping over to my bedside. Immediately, I returned the gun to its hiding spot. Then balled up into the same fetal position I had been in for the past week.

"I'll be alright," I murmured.

"Can I bring you anything?" He desperately wanted to alleviate my pain but it was useless. Unless he could bring my son back to life, there was nothing he could do for me. As Do It continued to talk, my mind drifted to the night Maine and I fled Detroit. I remember it like it was yesterday.

We were on the chartered jet heading away from the city that raised me. Something just didn't feel right. I thought it may have been the fear of getting caught. My mind told me not to worry because the worst was over. The private aircraft had been in the air for two hours already. We were in the clear.

"Maine, I'm not feeling well." I grabbed my stomach to soothe the shooting pains.

"Maybe you should lay back and close your eyes." He held my hand, yet continued to gaze out of the small window in deep thought. Part of me wondered what was on his mind. *Was it Nikki?* I thought silently but let it go. We were on our way to Mexico. Far away from her and any hold she may have had on him. She was no longer a threat to me.

"Baby, are you okay?" I asked.

"I'm just tired." He rubbed his face then readjusted himself on the cream colored leather seat.

"Get some rest then. I'm going to the bathroom." The pain in my stomach wouldn't let up. Maybe I needed to do number two and didn't know it.

The second I stood up, my legs became saturated with fluid. Slowly reaching between my thighs, I nearly gasped when I saw the slimy, clear fluid, and bloody mixture.

"Something is wrong! I need help!" Instantly, both Maine and Coco were out of their seats and attending me.

"Shit! I think your water just broke." Coco dropped to her knees, peering between my legs.

"Oh my God!" I screamed and doubled over in pain. Something felt as if it was falling outta my vagina.

"Lovely, lay down." Coco instructed and I did. She lifted the hospital gown above my waist then went into panic mode. "Maine, we need to land this plane A.S.A.P. She is about to deliver this baby."

"Shit!" Without delay, Maine approached the cockpit. He urged the pilot to land. Unfortunately, we were flying over the Gulf of Mexico and there was no landing strip nearby. "Don't worry baby, just hold on!"

"I can't hold on. He's falling out of me." I wasn't even pushing; the baby kept oozing out.

"Lovely, you'll be okay. I'm gonna try to deliver my godson, okay." Coco smiled and went to work between my legs. I lay there in shock at what was happening. Never did I envision delivering my son on an airplane. In contrast, it sure beat having him in prison. "What's his name going to be?" She asked to divert my mind from what was occurring.

"I want to name him Nazier," which is Maine's middle name. It wasn't an average name and sounded distinguished. I had big dreams for my little prince that didn't involve the street life or dope game. He was gonna be a doctor or a lawyer if I had anything to say about it.

A few minutes later, I felt my son make his exit from my body and into the world. I cried; I had done it! He was finally here. After spending my entire pregnancy behind bars and fearing having to give up custody of my son, it was finally over. We were heading into new territory and moving forward with our newfound life. After having endured so much tragedy, with my son and Maine by my side, the sky was the limit. "Let me hold him." I wiped my tears away. Closely, Coco held onto my tiny bundle of joy and rocked him slightly.

She was crying, so was Maine. Eventually, I recognized they weren't tears of joy; both of them were shedding tears of sorrow. "What's wrong!?" I screamed, now noticing that my son hadn't uttered a sound. *Weren't babies supposed to cry?* "Why isn't he crying!?" I yelled.

"I'm so sorry Lovely." Maine kneeled down and cradled me.

"Sorry for what? Let me see him." I pushed him off of me and fought hard to sit up. Reluctantly, Coco handed the tiny bundle over. I lost my breath.

My son was stillborn. His lifeless body was still connected to mine by the umbilical cord. Frantically, I placed my mouth to his and blew–it was useless. He was in Heaven while I was stuck in hell. I wasn't sure what I'd done to deserve the hand I'd been dealt. One thing was certain, I was tired of losing.

"Lo, did you hear me? I asked if you were alright. Do you need anything?" Do It snapped me out of my miserable mental space.

"I'm fine."

"I brought someone to see you." He went back over to the bedroom door, opening it wider. My niece, Shawnie was standing there with a huge snaggletooth smile.

"Auntie L, I made you something!" She waltzed her six-year-old self into the room then flopped down onto my king-size bed.

What did you make me baby?" I sounded more chipper than I actually felt.

"It's a get-well soon card." She showed me the card she had created with crayons and construction paper. A few words were misspelled but it was beautiful nonetheless.

"Thank you! It's so thoughtful!" I kissed her cheek.

"I just don't want you to be sad anymore." She leaned down, hugging me tightly.

"Auntie L needs some rest. Let's come back and check on her later." Do It pulled Shawnie from the bed; she reluctantly left.

Chapter Five
Nikki

"Look, Robyn is my sister, my blood sister." Roscoe explained as I tapped my foot impatiently waiting for him to finish the story. "Growing up, she was much younger than me so we didn't hang out. I took to the street life. She took the high road and became a police officer."

"So you knew the bitch was a cop and you still allowed her to infiltrate our organization?"

"By the time she was on the scene, I was behind bars doing that five year bid. I had no idea Nikki; I swear to God!" He raised his right-hand toward the sky.

"Whatever nigga!" I smacked my lips. Not believing for one second that Roscoe didn't know what his own sister was up to. "Finish the story."

"Anyway, while behind bars, I reached out to her and told her I was ready to clean up my act. In exchange for freedom, she asked for my assistance. At the time, I didn't know she was undercover with y'all. It wasn't until she told me about the shipment Mario was delivering to Zeke that I figured shit out." He paused before continuing. "I ain't gonna lie, I had plans to rob that fucking truck." The mere mention of the truck I was driving when I was shot brought back bad memories.

"So what happened? Why did you send Tonya to do it?" His baby mother was a pain in the ass. If she had not died before I was released from the hospital, I would've killed her my damn self.

"I didn't send Tonya to do it Nik. Actually, I had no idea she was even in the vicinity when that shit went down." He looked back at his children who were still standing over Chloe's casket. They were playing a game of Rock, Paper, Scissors.

"In the vicinity!? Nigga, Tonya tried to kill me!" I exclaimed, causing Junior to wiggle in my arms.

"She didn't even pull the trigger." He defended ole girl.

"Somebody shot me Roscoe! If it wasn't you, and it wasn't Tonya, who was it?" I looked at him sideways when he pointed toward the casket. "What? Are you saying Chloe shot me?"

"That's exactly what I'm saying." His bobbed his head up and down. "I will always have love for my baby sister but she was dirty. She took me out the game by staging my murder and putting me in witness protection. She tried to kill you and she bodied Tonya," he whispered.

"What!?" I was stunned with information overload. "How do you know all of this?"

"I found all of that shit out after she went to jail for murdering that other cop. All of her secrets fell out the closet," he sighed.

"Damn!" I didn't know what else to say. I was at a loss for words. More so, I was pissed beyond belief. I would've kicked over that damn casket had it not been morally wrong. How could my "friend" do me so dirty? All week I've been shedding tears over this bitch only to learn we were never friends in the first place. Mario was right!

"I only came back here because she's my sister. I also had to see if it was really her in that casket and not one of her tricks." Roscoe looked back at his children who were now sitting next to Mina talking her ears off.

"Well I can attest to the fact that your sister is really dead. She killed herself during a stand-off with police," I sighed. "She was six months pregnant with your niece."

"Robyn has a daughter?" I could tell he was elated, yet saddened by the news.

"She's at Children's Hospital."

"Wow!" He shook his head. "Do you have a picture or something?"

"As a matter of fact, I do." I scrolled down the photo gallery then showed him the only picture I'd taken of the miniature baby in the incubator.

"Look at how tiny she is." He stared at the photo.

"Her dad is at the hospital if you want to go visit her for awhile."

"No, I only came for the funeral." He handed me back the phone. "I have too many enemies in this city. I can't run the risk of being spotted."

"What happened to the witness protection?"

"After Robyn did what she did, they dropped me and my kids like a bad habit. We're out here on our own but it's all good. As long as we're together then we'll be alright." He called out for his children. "Come on, we 'bout to go." They stopped playing and ran over to his side. "It was good seeing you Nik. Tell the big homie I didn't mean for this to happen."

I hadn't planned on going to visit Mario today. However, after running into Roscoe, I was bursting at the seams to spill the tea. Upon accessing the private room, I spotted a nurse doing more flirting than actual patient care. She pretended to check Mario's vitals while feeling all over his body. Except for a pair of Hanes boxer briefs, he was lying there with nothing on. Previously, I had appealed to him to please keep the hospital gown on. Saying it cramped his style, he refused. I didn't know what style he was trying to uphold in a hospital but now

I see. Mario noticed my presence, "I knew you couldn't stand being away from a nigga for a whole day." His cocky ass looked up with a big smile. The nurse was obviously upset that I had ruined her play. Who cares, what I had to say was important.

"Is this your sister?" The nurse smugly asked to irritate me.

"No, that's my fuckin' wife standing there with my son," Mario barked.

"Oh, I'm sorry. Mrs. Wallace, I'm Brittani. Nice to meet you." She changed her tune so fast I caught whiplash.

"Please excuse us," I demanded.

"Um..." She stalled. "I wasn't finished with Mr. Wallace."

"Bitc..."

"Give us ten minutes." Mario cut me off before the rest of the word could leave my lips. She looked as if she wanted to say something but knew better.

"Look at you getting all jealous." Mario smirked after his nurse was out the door.

"Don't flatter yourself playboy. I only came by to tell you who I saw today." I placed Junior on the bed with Mario.

"You look good in that tight ass dress." He grabbed his manhood. Even in the hospital, Mario was a horndog. "You should let me get some real quick."

"Seriously Rio, listen to me!" I stomped my foot.

"I am serious girl. A nigga is in need."

"If you don't let me talk, I'm leaving."

"After you talk, can I hit it?" He raised his eyebrows multiple times and I cracked up laughing.

"Anyway, I saw a ghost today. His name is Roscoe."

"Roscoe who?" He was puzzled.

"Your old partner, Roscoe. Tonya's baby daddy, Roscoe." I reminded him, taking a seat on the chair beside his bed.

"Bullshit!" Mario bellowed.

"Square biz," I smirked.

"Where at?" He turned the television to the Disney Channel for Junior then gave me his undivided attention.

"He showed up at Chloe's funeral."

"How the fuck is a dead nigga gon' show up to a funeral?" Mario asked.

"I said the same thing but it was him. I even went up and talked to him. Dude had some very interesting things to say."

"Like what?"

"Well for starters, he told me Chloe was his

biological sister, and she placed him in the Witness Protection Program. He also told me she was the one who shot me." I sat back and watched his facial expression change from confused to pissed.

"Are you fucking kidding me!?" He yelled so loud I jumped. The monitor attached to his chest began beeping erratically as his heart rate rose. "I swear on my kids, if that bitch wasn't already dead, I'd kill her with my bare hands."

"I can't believe it either." Finally processing the facts, I shook my head. I trusted Chloe, treated her like a sister, and the bitch had the nerve to try and body me. It's because of her that I lost my family, almost lost my life, and was left with this limp.

"Where is that nigga, Roscoe at now?" Mario reached for his phone.

"What are you doing?" Right away, I became alarmed.

"It's time to lay that bitch ass nigga down for real!" Mario was furious.

"Rio, let him be. He has his children with him; and he's all they've got."

"Fuck that! You think I'm just gon' let a nigga come through and tell you all that shit then live to see tomorrow?"

"Baby, I'm okay. Please let him be. He had no idea Chloe worked for us because he was behind bars at the time."

"Bullshit!" Mario proceeded to dial the numbers on his phone.

"Rio, please just let that man be. He's just a brother wanting to say goodbye to his sister. Chloe was the problem and she's no longer a threat." Slowly, I placed my hand over his and removed the phone.

"What type of man would I be to let this shit ride?" He rubbed his temples.

"One that trusts me," I smiled. "Baby, every battle ain't worth fighting."

"I guess you're right." He placed the phone down on the nightstand near his bed.

"Are you guys finished?" The nurse was back. I started to tell her hell no we weren't finished, but I needed to leave anyway.

"Yeah, I was just about to go." I grabbed my son from the bed.

"Nik, where you going?" Rio asked.

"I've got to head home to finish writing my book."

"You really wanna be a writer, huh?" He smirked. Ever since I came out of my coma, I've had this compulsion to tell my story. Many people believe the dope game provides the glamorous life without consequences. Sure, I got to attend the best parties, spend obscene amounts of money, and never went to work a day after I said I do. Conversely, constantly worrying over when the police would kick the door in, or when the enemy would catch us slipping, was not a good feeling. If I can prevent one woman from following in my footsteps, then mission accomplished.

Chapter Six
Mina

I couldn't believe all the shit I heard while eavesdropping at the funeral. Chloe was something else; I couldn't wait to tell Sam.

"How was the funeral?" He asked after I stepped into the car. His eyes were bloodshot red. It was apparent he had been crying.

"Are you okay?"

"I'm good." He nodded then started the engine.

"Sam wait." I placed my hand on his to keep him from putting the car in drive. "Let's talk about it."

"I don't wanna talk about it. I just want to get back to the hospital with my daughter." Ignoring my request, he put the car in gear anyway.

"It's ok to be sad about Chloe." I knew exactly what was bothering him. "She was your ex-girlfriend and the mother of your child. It's natural to display emotion."

"I'll be alright; I'm just angry." He gripped the steering wheel and headed into the flow of traffic.

"Why are you angry?" My voice was yielding. I didn't want to come off like an interrogator.

"Look, let's just leave it alone." He brushed me

off.

"Sam, if we're going to be married one day, we have to learn how to communicate."

"Fine Mina," he relented. "I'm angry because I felt I should've done more. I also feel guilty because she took the murder wrap for what I'd done." For a brief second, he looked out the window. "Chloe wouldn't be dead if I wouldn't have killed your husband." His shoulders dropped as if he had been carrying the weight of the world on them.

"So this is my fault?" I was outdone. Nobody asked him to kill Tre. The murder was entirely his idea.

"Did I say that?" Not once did his eyes make contact with mine.

"You didn't have to," I sighed from annoyance.

"You see that shit right there is why I didn't want to fuckin' talk in the first place. Females always say they wanna talk, but when a nigga open his mouth and start spittin' that real shit, y'all feelings get hurt." He was upset.

"My feelings aren't hurt," I lied.

"Why are you pouting then?"

"I'm not pouting Sam." I lied again not wanting him to know how I really felt. In the back of my mind, I was aware that one day he would toss what he did for me back in my face.

"Chloe wasn't perfect but she didn't deserve that shit." He mumbled. It was time to shut this Chloe business down.

"Her brother attended the funeral today." I let my words linger in the air.

"Her brother…What brother?"

"His name is Roscoe. You might know him. He worked for the H.O.F. organization." I watched as a hint of familiarity came over his face. "He said she was the one who actually tried to kill Nikki."

"Are you sure?" He studied me for any signs of uncertainty.

"I was right there when he confessed to Nikki."

"Ain't this a bitch!" He said more to himself than to me. Feeling satisfied that his bubble had been burst, I reclined back in my seat with a smirk.

We rode in silence all the way to Children's Hospital. It wasn't until Sam maneuvered into a parking spot that he broke the deadly silence. "Baby, I'm sorry." He grasped my chin to turn my face toward him. "It's not your fault and it's not mine either. She put the gun to her own head and pulled the trigger."

"It's all good." I grabbed my purse then stepped from the vehicle. Internally, I was still seething but decided to drop the matter. Little Samantha needed us right now.

Chapter Seven
Gucci

"What up Gucci." Hassan the Arab gas station attendant spoke through the triple thick bulletproof glass. "Muhammad is waiting for you in the back."

"Fa sho." I grabbed a bag of barbeque Better Made potato chips and a grape Faygo pop before heading through the employee entrance. The gas station on the corner of Fenkell was one of my favorite traps. It was so low key that no one would ever guess we pushed pounds of cocaine through the back each month. It was like a workshop and everything ran smoothly. One of the transporters would deliver precooked cracked to the gas station in cleaning supply boxes. Then Muhammad would load the shit into merchandise boxes and distribute them to the other family owned gas stations. The money would come back the same way. I had no complaints.

After stepping through the employee entrance, I was greeted by an Arab wearing a turban with a gun. "Who the fuck are you?"

"Who the fuck are you?" I had never seen his ass before. It was evident he didn't know the chain of command.

"She's fine Ishmael." Muhammad placed a cell

phone into his back pocket then greeted me with a hug. "So nice to see you again.

"Muhammad, your boy here almost caught a hot one." While hugging my friend, I mugged Ishmael.

"This is my cousin, he's new. Please forgive him," he smiled. "Come have a seat while I get what you came for." He ushered me over to a computer desk and chair. I took a seat and made small talk while he was getting my bread. I liked Muhammad. He was cute in his own way. He wasn't your average Arab; he was more new school. He dressed in hip hop gear and wore more chains than some rappers. Had it not been for his crooked nose, stained teeth, and body odor, I would've introduced him to one of the girls from the Doll House.

"Yo homie, when you gon' take me for a spin in the new Mulsanne Bentley?" While behind the desk, I occasionally glanced at the security monitors. The new car was candy apple red with black rims and a custom black grill.

"You like it?" He poked his head around the wall safe. He was sending the cash through a money machine. I could hear the distinct sound. It was music to my ears.

"Hell yeah, I wish I could get one."

"Boss lady, you can get one without a doubt," he laughed.

"If I got one, the feds would be all over me." Most Arabs had racks on top of racks. A lot of Arab families owned gas stations, grocery stores, and other establishments. It was nothing for one of them to be riding around in expensive cars. The feds were too busy watching us to pay any attention to them.

"Do you want to drive it?" He asked, poking his head around the safe again. "The keys are in my drawer.

"No, I'll save it for next time." I twisted the cap off the pop then took a swig. There was nothing like a cold, grape Faygo.

"Where is the boss?"

"You're looking at her." I knew he was referring to Mario but I had nothing to say about him. Both Muhammad and I laughed.

"Well here you are my friend. Three hundred grand, in all big bills." He placed the duffle bags on the desk, waiting for me to count it, but I knew it was all good. We've been doing business with him for over eight years. Never once has his money come up short. Beside that, he was good people.

"'Till next time then." I stood for a hug then grabbed the heavy bags with all of my might.

INDIA

Chapter Eight
Lovely

I was awakened by the sunlight intruding into my dreams. "Baby, you have to get up from here." Maine had pulled the blinds back to reveal the beautiful private beach with crystal clear blue water. There was also a view of the Mesoamerican Reef in the distance. Regrettably, the scenery did nothing for me. Our secluded property in the Mexican Caribbean was spectacular on every level. Be that as it may, I had no desire to explore beyond this bedroom.

"Maine, please just leave me alone!" I didn't mean to snap but I was tired of people telling me what to do or how to feel. From the time the plane landed, everyone has given me the "time will heal all wounds" or the "you can't dwell in sorrow" speech. Until a mutha fucka has walked in my shoes, they have no right to tell me shit!

"Baby, I'm not leaving you in here for another day. It's been two weeks already. It's unhealthy for you to stay locked in here like this." He took a seat on the chaise beside the bed.

"What's unhealthy is losing a child!" I snapped.

"You think you're the only one hurting?" His

jaw muscles tightened. "He was my son too!"

"You didn't carry him for nine months Jermaine, I did." I pointed at my chest.

"So that makes my pain less significant?" He stood.

"I'm not saying that!" I snapped again.

"Sounds like it to me." He headed to the door. "This should be a time when we pull together and comfort one another. Instead, you're so wrapped up in your own feelings you're being too selfish to think about my grief!"

"Maine don't go there." I really didn't want beef between us but it was what it was. Our relationship had already been tested on too many levels. I realized we couldn't survive too many more blows. All the same, I was feeling confrontational. "Selfish is the last thing anyone should ever call me. Just get the fuck out!"

"Oh I'll leave, don't worry!" He went into the closet and slipped into a pair of shoes. "When I'm gone, don't try to find me either!"

"I won't!" I screamed. "We need some space any fuckin' way!" I don't why I said that. Honestly, there was too much space between us already. Sorrowfully, it was too late to take it back.

"Lovely, in my heart I know you don't mean that. But I don't know what else to do. All I want is for you to be happy." He paused and his shoulders dropped. "If my leaving makes you happy, then so be it. I can't watch you sulk around here day in and day out anyway."

I wanted to stop him; I allowed my pride to get in the way. He was the man of my dreams; and I was letting him walk out of my life like a stranger. Maine has been with me through the loss of both of my sisters, my father, my friend, and our son. We've been on the run from the law more times than I'd like to recount. Each and every time, he has proven to me he had my back. I don't know why I was so angry with him. It wasn't his fault our son died.

"I'll be gone for awhile. Do It and Shawnie are here if you need them. The rent is paid and there's money in the safe should you need it. When I come back, I hope it's not too late to save us." He approached the bed for a kiss. I turned my head in the other direction.

"See you later." The words were cold and I knew it. Silently, I resented him for giving up on me, although I had given up on my damn self.

"Damn, it's like that?" You said that shit as if I was running to the store or some shit." He shook his head then left the room without another word.

INDIA

Chapter Nine
Nikki

Two days after Chloe's funeral, I stepped into Salon 3k for my weekly appointment. All eyes were on me. The attention was nothing new to me but this was overboard. "Hey Nikki." Cynthia the receptionist spoke. She was new to the shop but good at her job. Baby girl could handle the phone lines, appointment book, and service the waiting area at the same damn time.

"Hey girl! What's going on around here?" Nothing went on without her knowing about it. For that reason, I knew she would fill me in.

"Girl, Gucci walked up in here about ten minutes ago. She's in the bathroom," she whispered.

"So why is everyone staring at me?"

"They're wondering if it's gonna be a catfight up in this piece." She stood from her seat then leaned in closer. "Coco ain't here yet but I can slide you into the breakroom before Gucci comes out."

"Girl, ain't nobody scared of her. I'll wait right here. Just let me know when Coco get's here." I walked pass two women talking out the side of their lips like I couldn't make out what they were saying. Reaching down to grab one of the Sister 2

Sister magazines, I heard the lady to my right whisper.

"You know she scared right?"

"You must not have heard what happened the last time them bitches saw each other. Nikki mollywhopped that ass!" The other lady replied.

"Yeah but then Gucci made a comeback at the hospital. I heard they was fighting all over Mario's hospital bed." She lied with a straight face. I wanted to correct her but there was no use. People in the hood were always gossiping about someone or something.

When Gucci approached the waiting area, everyone got so quiet you could hear a mouse piss on cotton. I wanted to show these bitches we were better than that. So I went over and sat next to her. "Hey Gucci how are you?"

"Nikkita!" She snapped and looked at me like I had no right to be near her. I was totally caught off guard and embarrassed. Had I known she was going to act like this, I never would've said anything.

"Look, I only came over here to see how you were and to ask about Maria." I stood calmly, trying not to cause a scene.

"Bitch, there's no need for you to be asking about me and mine!" She popped off at the mouth.

I had tried to be grown about the situation but she blew it. WHAP! I slapped her right in the face.

"I don't know what your problem is but you need to get that shit together." I swung with the left hand but she blocked it then came with a punch to the stomach. I doubled over to protect my stomach. That's when she came with a knee to my face. Luckily, I saw the move and dodged it.

"Come on bitch! Don't run now." She followed me toward the receptionist desk. I reached back, grabbed the cordless phone from its cradle, and caught that bitch right in the face.

"That's enough!" Coco was now in between us.

"Fuck that! This bitch thinks she's so tough, let her bang." Gucci barked.

"I've whipped your ass too many times this year. I'm done playing with little girls," I laughed.

"Your man didn't think I was a little girl when he was digging my guts out did he?" She intended for that to be a low blow. Yet, I found it amusing.

"He also didn't think the shit was good. You see who he came back to!" The crowd burst into laughter.

"Whatever bitch! Next time, I got a nine millimeter with your name on it."

"They didn't stop making guns when they made yours!" I retorted.

"You don't even know how to pop a pistol," she smirked.

"You'd be surprised."

"Come on Nikki. Let me do your hair." Coco attempted to halt the confrontation.

"Actually, I'll reschedule. All of a sudden, I have no need to be in the company of hoodrats." The comment was meant for Gucci as well as the crowd of onlookers.

Chapter Ten
Gucci

That bitch was back on my shit list! She'd been let off the hook too many times. Sooner or later, I was gonna snap, crackle, and pop all over her ass. "Gucci, are you ready?" My stylist asked after the commotion died down.

"Yeah." I nodded and followed her to the back of the swank salon.

"Girl that shit was crazy up there." She wrapped a cape around my neck then led me to the shampoo sink.

"What's crazy is I let her get away with that shit." Just thinking about it pissed me off again.

"Girl, don't trip over that syditty bitch." She smacked her lips. "You got her man and she's mad."

"I'm not with Mario anymore." I didn't miss the whispers and smirks from those around me. They would surely spread the gossip throughout Metro Detroit but fuck it. "I got a new nigga," I lied. I was as single as a one dollar bill but she didn't need to know it.

"Oh yeah! Who is this mystery man?" She turned the faucet on, adjusting the water temperature.

"That don't matter. Just know he's a boss!" I placed my head under the water and thought about Cartier. I hadn't heard from him since the day he took me to the hospital to see Mario. He said something came up and he had to make a trip out-of-town. That was almost two weeks ago.

After my hair was dried and styled, I decided to stop by the Doll House. I hadn't been by the club in a while. It was time to show my face. "What up Gucci." Taz, the bartender waved. She was a cute girl with dark brown skin, slanted eyes, and a body to die for. Frequently, I approached her about working as a dancer. However, she was too shy.

"Hey girl, let get me a shot of that white Remy on the rocks." Normally, I liked to mix my white Remy with Sprite but today I needed it straight up.

"You can pour your own trouble." She handed me a glass and the bottle of alcohol. It was Monday afternoon. The place wasn't crowded. Therefore, I took a seat atop one of the red bar stools.

"You want a drink?" I wasn't one for drinking alone–that shit was depressing.

"If you don't mind, then I don't mind." She grabbed the Ciroc Red Berry bottle and poured a double shot. "What's on your mind?"

"Why something gotta be on my mind to have a drink?" I tossed the shot back then poured another.

"Because you're at the bar on a Monday talking to me," she giggled. "Seriously though, what's wrong?"

I looked her over thoroughly and contemplated telling her my business. She was cool and all but I didn't really know her like that so I kept it simple.

"Girl, I'm cool. I needed to come here for some paperwork. Might as well have a drink in the process, right?"

"Umm Hmm." Her lips twisted up. "Is it about Mario?"

"What makes you say that?" I downed the second shot then poured a third.

"Word on the streets is he got back with Nikki." She slowly sipped from her glass.

"Fuck Mario!" I spat. Behind my anger was hurt and resentment. I wanted him to feel my wrath; I just had to wait until the time was right.

"Gucci, I hope I don't offend you with what I'm about to say," she paused.

"Depends on what you're about to say," I laughed.

"The best way to get over one man is to get up under another one," she giggled.

"I'll drink to that." I tossed back the third shot

and wiped the excess liquid from my mouth. The effect of the potent beverage was beginning to take its toll on me. I spent another hour kicking it with Taz before a surprise visitor showed up.

"What up Gucci. Let me holla at you right quick." Sam tapped me on the shoulder.

"Nigga, whatchu doing here?" My words ran together as I tried to get up from the barstool.

"I was riding pass and spotted the pink Charger on twenty-eights." He laughed and helped me get up. I told Taz I would be back and showed Sam into my office.

"So what's up?" I took a seat behind the desk.

"I got a problem," he sighed.

"Me too!" I smiled but he was serious.

"Man, I need to get put on with the organization again." He took a seat in one of the leather chairs across from me.

"Have you talked to Mario about this?"

"Not yet. Nikki got the hospital sowed up. Ain't no street business coming through there as long as she got anything to do with it." The mention of her name had me ready to vomit.

"I thought you were done with the dope game. What happened?" Sam was good at what he did. Although he would definitely be an asset to me, I needed to know why he wanted back in.

"I got into some shit and I need the extra bread." His eyes rested on mine. For the first time, I noticed how fine he was. Tall as hell and covered in tattoos–just the way I like 'em.

"What type of shit?" I took him in from head-to-toe and couldn't help but wonder how big his dick was. Maybe it was the liquor but I was suddenly turned on by his presence.

"Something personal that's all."

"Does Mina know?" I studied his face for a reaction.

"She don't need to know everything."

Now it could've been my imagination, but there was something in the delivery of his words that caused me to believe he was talking about more than selling drugs.

"You're right! She doesn't need to know everything." I rose from my seat then stood in front of the desk.

"So am I in or what?"

"I can you put back on no doubt. But you gotta do something for me first." I sat atop the desk and crossed my legs.

"What's that?" He played dumb. I could see the nigga's joint pulsating through the cargo shorts.

"I'm in need of a good fuck! Can you provide that for me?"

"Are you serious?" He stuttered.

"Do I look like I'm joking?" I opened my legs wide enough for him to see the pink thong.

"What about Mario?"

"What about him?" I slid one leg out of my underwear.

"What about Mina?"

"What about her?" I pulled him up close to me. The scent of Armani cologne was mesmerizing.

"Gucci, I can't." He shook his head. I wanted to tell this boy to stop being a bitch. Instead, I unzipped his pants. His penis was the size of a large Chiquita banana, curve and all.

"I won't tell if you don't." Licking my lips, I watched him ponder my proposition.

"You got a condom?" He pulled my legs up over his shoulders, laid me back, then he took me places I could only dream of.

Chapter Eleven
Mina

"Aye ma, you need a ride or something?" The client I'd just shown a fifty thousand dollar fixer-upper asked. We were smack dab in the middle of the hood, somewhere near Finney High School. I was nervous but kept it cool. My whip was in the shop so I'd been bumming a ride to and from showings with Sam. Normally, he stayed with me but today my clients wanted to see five homes. I told him to drop me off so he could go check on Samantha. He was supposed to be here thirty minutes ago.

"No thank you. I'm good." I smiled to mask the aggravation I was presently experiencing.

"Are you sure? It gets a little rough out here at night." He didn't have to remind me. I had already removed my jewelry, stuffing the items into my bra. Currently, I wished I could've concealed my purse but it was entirely too large.

"She said she was sure! Come on Clyde, damn." Benita, his impatient wife yelled. She wasn't an easy customer to please; I was happy to see her go. All day, I had to hear about granite countertops this and crown molding that. I wanted to tell that bitch she was ballin' on a budget.

Together, the two of them had only managed to snag a fifty thousand dollar FHA loan, which wouldn't buy you shit these days but a mediocre house at best. Clyde worked for the department of transportation and Benita was a stay at home wife. They wanted to live the lifestyle of the rich and famous on a beer budget.

"I guess we'll call you this weekend." Clyde smiled. "I think the third time is the charm."

"How about the two of you go home and take a look at the website. If you see anything that appeals to you *and* it's in your budget call me." I was not about to waste another Saturday with the likes of these two. Casually, I pulled out my cell phone then placed it to my ear.

"I told you we should've hired that other realtor." I could hear Benita attempting to whisper on the way to the car parked at the end of the driveway. "This bitch ain't even got a car. How can we expect her to have some class?"

I wanted to let Mrs. Benita know a thing or two but brushed the comment off. Getting Sam on the phone was a more pressing matter than her remark.

"The voicemail you are trying to reach has not yet been set up."

"Damn!" I ended the call, contemplating my next move. There was a gas station a few blocks from here. To get there meant I had to go through the trenches of the hood. Being unfamiliar with my surroundings, I decided to stay put and call Gucci.

"Hey Mina!" She sounded funny.

"Thank God you picked up! Where are you?" I jumped as a stray cat scurried from the bushes beside me.

"At the club, why?"

"I need a ride from the east side. Sam was supposed to be here awhile ago. It's getting dark now and a bitch is paranoid." I tried to make light of the situation. In all sincerity, I was scared for real.

"Text me your location and I'll be on the way." She ended the call.

Just as the sun was beginning to set, a gang of men came walking down the street. Instantly, my heart fluttered. I wanted to cross the street but that would've raised suspicion. As an alternative, I took a seat on the porch, pretending I lived there. "Ooh wee! Look at what Santa done dropped off in the ghetto." One of the men whistled.

"Christmas must've come early." Another fist bumped the other. "What's your name baby?"

"My name is Terri." I really wanted to ignore them and pray they passed quickly but I knew better. It was more of them than it was of me.

Sometimes ignoring them triggered an undesirable reaction.

"Terri, I ain't ever seen you before. Where you from?" The little one came up the walkway. I felt my stomach drop. Why didn't he just keep it moving?

"I'm from Ohio." That part was the truth. "I'm visiting a friend. She'll be here any minute," I rambled.

"Dorothy, you ain't in Kansas no more." He teased. The crowd busted up laughing. "This is Detroit bitch! Come off them Red Bottoms. Give me that cell phone and I want that purse!" He demanded. Out of nowhere, he was brandishing a handgun.

Slowly, I slipped out of my shoes, handed over the purse, and cell phone. The young thief took my shit and got ghost.

Chapter Twelve
Lovely

I lay in bed contemplating my next move. Maine had been gone for almost a day and hadn't bothered to call home. I hadn't called him either so we were even. It was so peaceful without him; I feared I was getting accustomed to it. *Knock. Knock.* The sound of the door concluded the staring contest I was having with the ceiling.

"Come in." Even though I wasn't up for company, I didn't want to turn Shawnie away if it was her. She'd been down to see me every day; I felt bad about not playing with her.

"Lovely baby, when are you coming out of this room?" Agent Nichols sauntered in wearing a hot pink track suit. Her voice was soft and gentle. As a result, it was difficult to snap at her, so I didn't. She was like the mother I never had but always dreamed of. The funny thing about our relationship was she was a retired FBI agent and I was a fugitive.

"No time soon." I rolled over to look at her.

"Girl, I can't let you lay up in here like this, waiting for death to come." She tugged at the covers.

"Death has to be better than this," I groaned.

"Baby, you've got it twisted." Her choice of words put a smile on my face. She was old school, so to hear her talking like the young folks was humorous. "Your life ain't over just because you lost a child. Trust me, I know." She pointed to her chest. Her daughter was killed by my father and his gang back in the eighties. The assassination was solely meant for the daughter's boyfriend. Dreadfully, she was in the wrong place at the wrong time. "My baby was grown. It was too late for me to start over. At least you're young. You've still got time."

"I don't have time." I sat up on the bed, folding my legs Indian style. "When we landed here, Maine rushed me to the local hospital. After they snipped the umbilical cord, examined me, and cleaned me up, a doctor came to see me. He informed me that my uterus was no good. My chances for carrying a baby to term are primarily non existent." It felt good to divulge the secret I'd been keeping. I hadn't shared this information with anyone.

"If your uterus is bad how did you carry a baby for nine months?"

"My son actually died during my second trimester and I didn't even know it. Regular prenatal check-ups would have caught it but the prison didn't offer extensive medical treatment."

"Lovely, I know doctors are supposed to be smart. Don't ever forget this - the person with the final say so is Jesus." She pointed toward the ceiling. "Everything is predestined. If it's meant for you to have a child then the Lord will give you one."

"I guess you're right but..."

"No buts Lovely. You must learn to have faith sweetheart." She patted my hand.

"I guess I do need to get up from here." Although everyone had said it dozens of times, Nichols was different.

"No, what you need to do is call that man of yours." She handed me the cordless phone she had in the pocket of her jacket then left me to make the call.

I dialed all seven digits with caution. I didn't know what to say. An apology wouldn't come easy. Still, I would do the best I could. After four rings, the call was sent to voicemail. "Jermaine it's me. I want you to come home so we can talk." I paused before ending the call to say I love you, but the words wouldn't come out. For some reason, they were stuck in the pit of my stomach. My heart was cold. Love was nothing but a four letter word–it meant nothing.

Chapter Thirteen
Nikki

"I can't believe I missed all that shit." Anj shook her head in disbelief. I was catching her up about all the latest drama with Gucci. We were having dinner at Benihana, her treat. She had settled the case in Los Angles out of court for an undisclosed amount. The reality star didn't want the nasty headlines the case was sure to create to prevent her from obtaining future gigs. Anjela flew back in last night with another notch in her belt.

"I'm going to kill that bitch!" I mumbled casually while watching the chef toss my egg into his hat then down onto the sizzling hot grill.

"I'll plan your defense strategy for court," she laughed. "I can't stand that ghetto rat."

"That makes two of us!" Shaking my head, I held the plate out for the chef.

"What's the news with her and Mario?"

"Truthfully, there is no news. Until today, she's been missing in action; and I like it that way." I attempted to use the chopsticks but failed miserably. "Rio is pissed that he hasn't seen Maria but it's no sweat off my back, especially after what happened earlier."

"Maybe that hoodrat will finally get a clue and

realize she can't replace you." Checking her phone, Anj replied to a message.

"I guess," I shrugged. "So besides the case, what's new? I feel like we haven't kicked it in forever." Although Anjela was my first cousin, we were more like sisters. My mother and her father were siblings. They both spent time in the streets which caused Anj and I to spend a lot of nights with our grandmother back in the day.

"I know right!" She was still texting on her phone with a smile.

"What in the hell are you smiling so hard for?"

"While I was in Los Angeles, I met a man." She put the phone down. "His name is Carter Jones. He's tall, fine as hell, and pretty well-off." Her phone lit up; she went back to texting. "He's a Federal Agent with the FBI." She beamed as I frowned. Although we were so much alike, our worlds seemed so different at times. Anjela was always into the nerdy, preppy type. Of course, I was into bad boys. "I see you frowning. He's not that bad."

"I hate the alphabet gang." Anjela understood it was code for the FBI, DEA, ATF, as well as the PO-PO.

"As long as you ain't doing nothing illegal then you ain't got nothing to worry about," she laughed.

"Could you imagine what Thanksgiving dinner would be like with him and Mario at the same table?" Just the thought alone had me cracking up.

"Uncomfortable as hell," she continued laughing. "Seriously though, you have to meet him one day. I know you'll like him."

"This sounds pretty serious cuz."

"I think it is," she beamed. "I haven't met a man that had me this open since Donald." The mention of her ex-lover had me in tears. "What's wrong with you?" She looked at me crazy while I was wiping my eyes. He was the goofiest looking thing I'd ever laid eyes on. His glasses were too big, the suits he wore were too small, and his teeth were too long, but Anjela loved him. That is, until his wife showed up one night at the hotel to claim her property.

"Don't take this the wrong way but you fuck with some ugly dudes. You're too damn cute for that." My cousin was a bonifide beauty with the brains and body to match.

"Forget you! Those ugly dudes come with big money that's legal." She winked. "You do the ballers and I'll stick with bankers."

"Now that was cold." I pretended to be offended. "Anyway, when can I meet his ugly self?"

"Keep it up and you won't get to meet him until the wedding," she giggled. "And for your ınformation, my man is not ugly." She grabbed her phone, showing me a picture of him sitting on a sofa reading the Wall Street Journal or something.

"Damn." The word escaped my mouth before I could stop it. The brother was fine; I had to give props. For some reason, he looked very familiar.

"Told you he wasn't ugly." She snatched the phone back. "He'll be in town next month; maybe you can meet him then."

"What's he coming for?" I was being nosey.

"He's looking into some old case files. Trying to tie up a few loose ends before the promotion he wants comes around."

"What kind of case files?" I tossed back the Saki. Japanese liquor wasn't the best but it sure did give you a buzz.

"The hell if I know," she shrugged.

"Well I hope Mario's name ain't on any of those files." It was meant as a joke but neither of us laughed.

Chapter Fourteen
Gucci

I pulled down the deserted street bumping French Montana looking for Mina. She wasn't answering her cell phone. I would've turned around if it weren't for the fact that I had already driven all the way over here. Letting up off the gas I dropped the car down to a slow speed. The street lights were on but it was hard as hell to see anything. I damn near hit a group of niggas who had darted out into the middle of the street. *Damn kids!*

I rode down three more blocks before spotting Mina standing on the porch of a house with a for sale sign out front. She looked scared as hell; I found it amusing.

"What took you so long?" She got in, slamming the door.

"I would've been here sooner if you would've answered your cell phone." Whipping the car into a u-turn I headed back in the direction I'd just come.

"They took my phone, my shoes, and my cell phone," she sniffed. For the first time, I noticed she was barefoot.

"Who?" I slammed on the brakes.

"Some dudes robbed me about ten minutes

ago."

"Mina are you okay?" I turned on the interior lights to inspect her for injuries.

"He had a gun," she cried. "He could've killed me."

"What did they look like?" There was a nine millimeter stashed behind the radio panel. I was prepared to bust a cap in someone's ass.

"I don't know but it was a bunch of them," she avowed.

"Was one of them wearing a red snapback?" I bet my bottom dollar it was those fuckers I just passed.

"Yeah, how did you know?" She stopped crying. I didn't say anything. Nonchalantly, I put the car back in gear and sped down the block. "Gucci where are we going?"

"I'm going to get your shit back." I didn't even look at her while I drove. I was on a mission.

A few blocks, and several corners later, I pulled up in front of a house on Houston-Whittier. "Is that them?"

"Yeah, but don't go up there," she cautioned.

"Girl, I ain't about to let some knuckleheads punk you." Pressing the code on the custom radio, I waited for it to unlock then grabbed my gun. "Are you coming?"

"No." She shook her head.

"Suit yourself. I'll be back."

The place looked decent with flowers out front and a freshly cut lawn. I knew it wasn't a trap; probably someone's mother's house. "Who dat?" One of the men tried to make me out in the darkness.

"It's Gucci." This might sound conceited as hell but everybody in Detroit either knew me or knew somebody who knew me.

"What you doing round these parts." Another one of the men stepped down onto the walkway. "You're from the H.O.F. organization right?" He smiled like we were friends. His lame ass was pretending for his boys. Wanting to get Mina's shit back, I played it cool.

"Yeah that's me. What's cracking fam." I went in for a dap. "My homegirl lost her purse. She says one of y'all found that shit along with her shoes and cell phone." Instantly, the smile disappeared. It was replaced by nervousness.

"Your girl said we found it?" He played dumb. "Fellas, y'all seen anybody purse round this bitch?"

Before they could co-sign his lie, I lifted my shirt so that he knew I was packing. "Look homey, I ain't come here for trouble. I just want my girl's shit and I'm gone."

"Gucci, I don't want it with you." He exhaled noisily, obviously contemplating the consequence of lying to me or snitching on his boy.

"I don't want it with you either. Looks like I got no choice." I shrugged and reached for my cell phone. He thought I was going for the strap and flinched. I pretended to dial a few numbers while resisting the urge to laugh. "Aye it's Gucci." I spoke into the phone. "I tried to be cordial and handle shit by my lonesome but it looks like I'm gonna need some reinforcement." As I spoke his eyes widened. He didn't really want no drama, none of them did. If these were real niggas, they would've pulled the gun they used on Mina on me.

"Just give the bitch her shit." I could hear someone on the porch whisper.

"I would hate to shoot up your mama's house over a handbag. But I've done a lot worst for less."

I watched him process what I said. As if a light bulb came on, homeboy hustled over to the crew. He was back in seconds with a purse, a cell phone, and a pair of Red Bottoms. "My fault Gucci. We didn't know she was your girl."

"No harm, no foul. You returned her shit that's all that matters." I retrieved the items, headed to the car, then swiftly turned around. "One last thing before I leave homey."

"What's that?" His guard was down.

"Run yo pockets now nigga!"

Chapter Fifteen
Mina

It was well pass eleven by the time Gucci dropped me off at home. Sam's car was in the driveway. I was seething. The moment I opened the door it was on. "Hey baby, I see you got a ride." He waltzed pass me with a bowl of ice cream.

"I had to call Gucci after your ass didn't show up." I hung my purse on the coat rack then bent to remove my shoes, only to find they were still in my hand. I hadn't bothered to put them back on.

"My bad. The reception at the hospital is bad. When I called you back, you didn't answer."

"I didn't answer because I didn't have my fucking phone! I was robbed!"

"Robbed?" He looked as if I were making shit up.

"Yes robbed! As in they took my shit at gunpoint!" Frustrated was beyond what I was feeling.

"Damn baby, are you okay?" He placed the ice cream down then grabbed me. The hug was just what I needed at the moment. It didn't exactly stop my anger but it did feel good. We hadn't been intimate since Chloe died. A sister could use some attention. This wasn't really the attention I had in mind but it was a good start.

"I'm fine. Gucci came to get me AND she got my shit back. That girl is a beast!"

"Oh." He stiffened up and backed away.

"What's wrong with you? Why are you acting strange?"

"I'm not acting strange." He picked up the bowl and continued eating.

"Anyway, what did the doctors say about Samantha?" I began to undress. It had been a long day. All I wanted was a bath and sleep.

"They said she's coming along just fine. We might get to bring her home in a month or so. They want her up to at least five pounds first."

"Great! I'll start working on the nursery sometime next week."

"Cool." He started to walk away.

"Hey, I wanted to talk to you about the wedding. Do you have time?" With his attitude lately I'd been ruminating over postponing it.

"What's up?" Sam hesitantly asked.

"I was thinking we should call the wedding off or postpone it, at least until we bring Samantha home and get situated with raising her." After I said it, I wanted to take it back. It was really meant as an attention grabber but it was too late.

"Actually, I was thinking the same thing." He

kissed my cheek.

"So you don't want to get married?"

"I do want to get married; I don't think right now is a good time." Sam headed up the stairs with me on his trail.

"So when will you be ready?"

"Mina, chill out. Two seconds ago you said you wanted to postpone the damn thing. Now you're mad because I agreed with you?"

"I only said it to get your attention. You didn't even protest."

"Are you on your period or something?" He frowned. I didn't even respond. Storming into the bathroom, I slammed the door.

INDIA

Chapter Sixteen
Lovely

After being gone for an entire week, seemingly, Maine had no intentions of coming home. He'd given up on us, thrown in the towel. I didn't even blame him because I'd done the same. There no use in trying to work shit out. Our relationship had run its course. I was okay with that or so I told myself. Candidly, it was another let down, a big disappointment, and a major waste of time. With him out of my life, the yearning to kill myself was overwhelming. There was nothing left to live for. My fight was over. I was ready to lay down my burdens and head into the afterlife. "Lo, where are you going?" Do It was playing Go Fish with Shawnie at the kitchen table.

"I need some fresh air. I'm going out for a few." I walked over to the table, hugged my brother, and then kissed my niece. They had no idea I was never coming back.

"Where are you going?" Do It laid his cards down then stood. He knew better.

"I'm going to walk along the beach."

"Oooh, can I go?" Shawnie jumped up and down.

"Yeah, let's take a family walk. I could use

some fresh air too." His eyes never left mine.

"Not this time guys. I need to do this alone." I headed toward the door before he could stop me. By the time Do It and Shawnie could slip on shoes, I'd be gone.

In my absence, I left a note lying on my pillow. It would explain everything. It was my hope they understood my rhyme and reason. Sometime tonight, either Do It or Nichols would find it. When they did, it would be too late. I'd already be well into the afterlife–be it Heaven or hell.

I walked down the dirt road for a mile until I saw a sign that read: Publica Playa. It meant public beach in Spanish. From a distance, I could see the aqua blue water. Like bath water, it looked calm and soothing. All I had to do was get in, close my eyes, and submerge myself. The water would fill my lungs and nostrils. In no time, my air supply would be depleted. Then I would drown and float away with the current.

As thoughts of death replayed in my mind, I was distracted by sounds coming from a bar further down the street. I wasn't familiar with the up-tempo melodies but decided to grab a drink to calm my nerves. Thankfully, the baggy sweatpants I borrowed from Maine's side of the closet housed a Ben Franklin. Although no one was paying me any mind, I felt uncomfortable upon crossing the threshold of the small shack. The bartender was shooting the breeze with a customer. A few people were in the middle of the floor dancing. Several others were in booths to themselves. "Hello, can I get a..." I paused. Nothing on the shelf was familiar.

"No hablo englis." He shook his head.

"Obtner la dama un trago de tequila." A gentleman approached the bar then sat beside me. I had no idea what he said but the bartender smiled, beginning to pour a drink.

"What did you say?" I asked the handsome stranger. He was gorgeous with jet black hair, tanned skin, and a crooked smile. It was cute in its own little way.

"I told him to get the lady a shot of Tequila," he winked. There was something about him that made my heart flutter. Self-consciously I smoothed the hair on my head, silently cursing myself for not looking more presentable. Even though I was about to die, I didn't have to look busted.

The bartender sat a shot glass before me and one in front of my companion. I nodded my head in appreciation before taking a sip of the gold liquid. "Como te llamas?" He asked. When I didn't respond, he translated the question into English. "What's your name?"

"I'm Lovely, and you are?"

"Me llamo Mauricio," he smiled. "Are you from here?"

"No. I'm from the United States."

"Are you on a vacation or something?" He never took a drink; he stared at me. I could've looked into his eyes all night. However, I was on a mission.

"Yeah." I lied then downed the remainder of my drink.

"Are you here with friends?" He searched the bar for possible acquaintances of mine.

"You sure do ask a lot of questions Mauricio." I was beginning to feel paranoid. It was time to go. "Thanks for interpreting my order. Have a round on me;" I slapped the one hundred dollar bill on the bar top then stood abruptly.

The affect of the alcohol hit me unexpectedly. My legs felt like cement. I fell over onto Mauricio. Something wasn't right. I attempted to speak but the only thing coming forth was gibberish. When I noticed the look exchanged between the bartender and Mauricio, I knew what the deal was. They had slipped me a ruffie.

Chapter Seventeen
Nikki

"It feels good to be back on the bricks!" Mario looked out the window as we drove down Livernois Avenue. "I never thought I would be so happy to see the streets of Detroit in my life!"

"God is good!" I'm not an avid churchgoer, nor am I your average Christian but I knew enough to give credit when it was due. Ms. Claudia and I had prayed for Mario's life, and he showed us favor. I'd heard once before that He moved mountains if you just trusted and believed. After witnessing what He brought me through I was a firm believer.

"Amen! God is good." My ex-husband repeated the saying. The streets had damn near killed us both but here we were alive and well.

"Amen daddy." Mario Junior repeated from the backseat; we cracked up laughing. It was good to be a family again. Sorrowfully, I was aware that the good times were nearing an end. It was time to face the reality that Mario was legally married to someone else as well as father to another child. Although Gucci had yet to make an appearance since the beauty shop brawl, she was unquestionably lurking around the corner.

"Where do you want me to take you?" I asked

after pulling up to the light.

"Take me to your house."

"Do you think that's a good idea?" I released the brake, putting the SUV back into motion. "You need time to clear your head and decide where you wanna be."

"Nik, I already know where I wanna be. Which is exactly where I'm at right now." He looked at me and winked.

"Well you need to clear the air with Gucci first. I'm not to trying to beef with that girl." I was done playing games with her. The next time she came for me would be the last time and I mean that."

"Oh please believe, I'm gonna clear the air." Mario huffed. He was pissed that Gucci hadn't brought Maria to visit him in the hospital. I understood his frustration. Conversely, as a woman, I identified with where she was coming from. She felt betrayed and rightfully so. Mario had played with her like a doll then placed her back on the shelf. She was hurt and wanted to hurt him just as badly. They were playing the dangerous game of love and war. Consequently, Maria was caught in the crossfire.

"What about the marriage?" The words tasted venomous rolling off my tongue.

"What about it?" He replied indifferently.

"In order for us to move forward, you have to divorce her."

"Knowing her, she probably already filed the paperwork," he laughed. "That broad probably done tore up my shit, bleached my clothes, and burned the house down by now."

"What about the H.O.F. organization? You're done with that right?" The question had been on my mind daily. I loved Rio but not enough to watch the streets slowly eat him alive, especially after we'd been given chance after chance to leave the street life behind.

"Nik, let's not visit that shit right now." He brushed the issue under the rug, turning up the bass on the stereo. I decided to give him a break on the subject for a week or two.

Pulling up to the home I purchased after our divorce, I cut the engine off. "You know we need to upgrade right?" He looked at me. "This place is small."

"Says the nigga who don't even have a house!" I countered while laughing.

"Oh, I have houses believe that!" He chuckled. "But seriously, we need a bigger spot before the baby comes." He went to rub my stomach and I swatted his hand. The mention of what was growing inside of me put a bitter taste in my mouth. I shuttered at the thought of having Maine's baby. I barely knew him and never planned on seeing him again. Having his child would only remind me of a poor choice I made in the heat of the moment. Therefore, abortion was the route I wanted to go but Mario was dead set against the idea. He swore to love the child as his own. Unfortunately, I had my reservations. This is why I hadn't completely written the idea off yet.

"Rio, take it easy!" I changed the subject when he hopped down from my SUV like a man who hadn't just been released from the hospital.

"Girl, I got this!"

"Excuse me, Mario Wallace may I have a word?" Some white man approached us with a recorder in his hand.

"Who are you?" Seemingly, he had materialized from the thin air.

"My name is Michael Jenkins. I'm a reporter with Detroit Dish doing a story on crime and our community." He pressed the record button. "Is it true that you are the force behind the Hand Over Fist crime organization?"

"What?" Mario mugged him. "Dude you got two seconds to get the fuck off my property!"

"Is it true that your organization has made millions of dollars in drug money?"

"One." Mario counted.

"I'm just…"

"Two." Mario reached under the grey Nike t-shirt for a gun that wasn't there. It was ploy to get the man away from us and it worked. Homeboy was in his car and speeding off before I knew it.

"I wonder what that was all about." I grabbed Junior from the backseat.

"I don't know, but he's the second dude to approach me about some damn newspaper story." He leaned up against the SUV to get his balance.

"Mario, let me help you." I put Junior down to walk then went over to assist Mario. The doctor said his sense of balance might be off for a few days.

"Girl, there's nothing wrong with me." He refused my assistance.

"Yeah mommy, there's nothing wrong with daddy." Junior cosigned.

"That's right son, you tell her I'ma boss!" He popped the invisible collar on the t-shirt he was wearing with Junior doing the same.

"Whatever."

Just as I unlocked the front door, Mario's cell phone rang. My stomach did a back flip. His phone had been off almost the entire time he was in the hospital. In addition to that, no one was allowed to visit except family and close friends, which kept that street shit far away from us. I knew the minute word spread he was back on the block, the damn phone would be ringing off the hook like crazy.

"What up fam?" He pressed the speaker button while taking a seat on the couch.

"What's crackin' my nigga! I heard you hit the bricks and shit. How you feelin' son?"

"I'm one hundred." Mario bent down to untie Junior's shoes.

"That's good." There was a pause. "You up for talking business?"

"I'm listening." Mario looked at me and I rolled my eyes. He knew I wasn't fond of that life anymore. For him, it was business as usual.

Chapter Eighteen

Gucci

Since my first rendezvous with Sam, he's been to my hotel several times to put in more work. I felt bad for sneaking behind Mina's back but a bitch had needs. Sam had a real thick pipe; it was long too. He knew what he was working with and used the curve well. I rationalized with myself that I wasn't doing my friend *real* dirty if I didn't fuck him raw or let him give me head. That shit right there just would've been disrespectful. Buzzz. The phone vibrated against the loose change at the bottom of my purse. It was a message from Sam that read: *Hey boss lady! I got some free time tonight. Would you like me to slide through and drop off that package?*

I thought about what plans I might've had tonight before responding: *Yeah I need that ASAP. See you at eight.* We spoke in code to throw Mina a loop if she ever came across the messages. When she read the word "package" she would relate it to dope. I dropped the phone back into my purse; it vibrated again. This time it was a call from Mario. "What?"

"For real G, it's like that?" He asked. I was holding the cell phone to my ear barely listening. I didn't have time for this nigga and his mood swings today.

"Like what nigga?" I snapped, causing the white sales clerk behind the jewelry counter to stare. "Let me see that right there." I pointed to a pair of chocolate diamond studs. The money I collected on the second of the month still had a bitch sitting pretty. I had been out splurging on me and Maria everyday. It was something about hitting a nigga in his pockets that did my heart some good. In fact, I thought that's why he was calling–I was wrong.

"Are you bringing my daughter over here or what?"

"Over where?" He had to be mistaken if he thought I would step within fifty feet of Nikki. "You got me fucked up!"

"Look, you ain't gotta bring her to me. Let me come and get her."

"No."

"What the fuck you mean no? That's my fucking daughter too!"

"I said no. What part didn't you understand the n or the o?" I placed the earrings up to my ear, admiring them in the oval mirror.

"You been acting real reckless lately Gucci! Don't let me see you in the streets 'cause when I do, it won't be pretty."

"I guess I'll have to worry about that when you find me then, huh?" I ended the call. Truthfully, I knew I was on borrowed time, which is why I moved out of the house and into a hotel days ago. When Mario finds out I took all the money we made on the second and spent it, he's going to have a fit. But he owed me. We hadn't been married long enough for me to take him to court. Because of that, I collect my shit in the streets. "I'll take these and the matching necklace too." I handed the earrings back to the clerk and waited for her to ring me up.

"That'll be fourteen thousand, two hundred, forty-seven dollars and sixteen cents." She smiled, pleased with her commission. Reaching into my purse, I was prepared to hand the lady my money when someone handed her a credit card. I turned to see Cartier standing there.

"Where did you come from?" I thought this fool was gone with the wind.

"I didn't follow you I swear." His hand rose toward Heaven. "I happened to be shopping over there when I saw you."

"Umm Hmm." I eyed him cautiously. "Where have you been?"

"I had to handle some business in California. Did you miss me?" He retrieved my bag from the sales rep then handed it to me.

"No I didn't but thank you for the gift."

"It's the least I could for splitting on you like that. My people called and I had to move fast. You could've at least called me though."

"I could've, but I was busy. Besides, the phone works both ways." I dropped the small shopping bag into my purse then pushed Maria's stroller out of the store.

"I wanted to give you and your man time to work things out." He followed behind me.

"I told you before there's nothing to work out." I strolled through Somerset mall with no destination in mind. Maria and I had just about cleaned the place out already.

"Good." He bent down to retrieve Maria.

"You say that like you got plans for me or something," I smiled.

"I do Gucci." He eyed me seductively. "I got plans to make you mine again."

"I ain't trying to be tied down anymore." I was only half joking. As fine as Cartier is and as good as his dick was, I wasn't feeling another relationship so soon. I needed some time to do me.

"I know your last nigga hurt you but he ain't me and I ain't him." He pleaded his case. "Me and you make magic in the streets and in the bedroom.

It's only fitting that we team up and take this shit to the next level." The way he cradled my daughter to his chest, for a quick second, caused me to wish she was his.

"So what exactly are you talking about?"

"Gucci, I'm about to take over the world, and I want you riding shotgun." The tone of his voice was serious. "I'm talking about Detroit…Miami… New York…Atlanta…St. Louis…and Las Vegas." He continued to plead his case. "I'm a movement by myself. Together, we're a force to be reckoned with. This thing will bring in more money than you knew existed."

"You know I'm all about the Benjamins." Hearing more money was music to my ears.

"Your mouth is saying one thing but your eyes tell a different story." He was so intuitive; I loved that about him. How many thugs do you know that actually give a damn about a woman's feelings.

"You're right," I affirmed. "Building an organization with you destroys the one I constructed with Mario."

"Let me get this straight. You're sad about putting your baby's daddy out of business?" He laughed hysterically.

"It's not about Mario. It's about the crew that I handpicked and taught the game. It's about the homeys I call my brothers." Regardless of what it looked like on the surface, at the core, the H.O.F organization was a family. "I could care less about shutting Mario down." I smacked my lips.

"Gucci, this game is treacherous. You can't wear your emotions on your sleeve. That shit will get you murked!" Cartier reprimanded. "In this day and age loyalty ain't shit but a seven letter word," he scoffed. "I bet you for the right price, anyone of them niggas you call your family will put your ass in a body bag, real talk." His words hit me in the pit of my stomach–they were true. I was attached to the organization and every individual associated with it. Sadly, things have changed. Maybe it was time to move on. "Look, if it makes you feel better, you can bring some of your crew over to our side."

"What would we name the organization?"

"I don't see why it can't still be known as the H.O.F. organization. I mean you do own half the name," he recommended.

"I guess that's true." In my head, the wheels were turning. I was on a mission to piss Mario off. This would definitely do the trick.

Chapter Nineteen
Mina

As I stepped into the Neonatal ward at Children's Hospital, I was greeted by one of Samantha's nurses. "She's doing so well mom."

"How much does she weigh now?" I sat my purse down then went over to the sink to scrub my hands. When dealing with sick babies with weakened immune systems, being sterile was the rule.

"She's up to three pounds and eight ounces," she smiled. "I told your husband she should be coming home really soon." The word "husband" felt like a dagger to my heart. It was a reminder that Sam didn't want to marry me. The fairytale I thought I was going to have was slowly becoming a nightmare.

"Yeah, we can't wait to bring her home." I smiled, walking over to the incubator.

Baby Samantha was sleeping as usual. She was so medicated with steroids for her lungs as well as other medications that she was rarely ever awake. I had yet to see her eyes for longer than a minute. I knew they were pretty though. "Hey mama." I slid my finger into one of the holes to caress her tiny thigh. She was laying there in a pink cap and diaper. Her face was covered in tubes. At times it was hard to stomach. "Samantha, I can't wait for you to come home. I'm gonna paint your room this weekend. Are you a pink or purple kind of girl?" I had already decided to use both colors. Talking to her was soothing to me. It reminded me of when I would talk to my own son. Sadly, he didn't make it pass a year. As a replacement, I felt God had given me Samantha. The funny thing is Samantha looked just like Chloe. That didn't matter, I loved her like she was mine.

"Would you like to hold her?" I'd forgotten the nurse was still standing there.

"Oh yes! Please!"

"Of course! Just slip this on over your clothes." She handed me something similar to a paper surgical outfit. "Ok, now have a seat and I'll hand her to you."

I did as instructed, watching her open the incubator like a wrapped present then hand me the gift inside.

"Here's your mommy."

"Oh my god she's so tiny." I blinked back a few tears. My hands were shaky because I feared I would drop her. "Will I hurt her?"

"She's strong, you won't hurt her." She stood nearby until I got comfortable enough to sit back.

For over an hour, I held unto baby Samantha for dear life. I talked to her and even hummed a few songs. It felt good to have a child in my arms again. In that moment, I vowed to love her, and protect her as if she were my own.

"Ma'am, I hate to disturb you but when your husband was here earlier, he left his phone." The nurse handed me Sam's phone.

"Thank you! He's always so careless with things like this."

INDIA

Chapter Twenty
Lovely

"Where am I?" I blinked rapidly. My vision was cloudy and I felt disoriented. We were in a car riding down a dirt road. Mauricio was behind the wheel, I was in the passenger seat with both my hands and legs tied.

"I'm taking you to your new home." His crooked smile no longer appealed to me. Moreover, he looked nothing like the handsome stranger I met in the bar. His brows were now furrowed and his demeanor was peculiar.

"Why are you doing this?" I tried to break free of the rope around my wrists–it was useless.

"You're just what I needed Lovely." He spoke without removing his eyes from the road. "My clients are gonna love you."

"What the fuck are you talking about?" At this point, I was more afraid than ever. What in the world had I gotten myself into? A few hours ago I had plans to kill myself now I was being kidnapped in a foreign country by a total stranger. "Answer me dammit!" Most likely, I shouldn't have taken such a tone. I didn't know what this man was capable of but I wasn't no punk either.

"No questions!" He veered off the road into a

private driveway.

The driveway led to a house just beyond a few corn stalks. It sat behind a ten foot steel gate with the initials S and M on it. The white stucco home was huge. It reminded me of a mansion you might see in a gangster movie. Guards surrounded the property wearing black suits and dark shades. "Beinvenido de nuveo." One of the guards opened up Mauricio's car door.

"Take her to the east wing with the others!" Mauricio instructed before walking away.

"What's happening to me? Please help!" I pleaded with the guard but he said nothing. Lifting me out of my seat, he carried me inside of the mansion kicking and screaming.

"Stop it!" He whispered. His voice wasn't as cold as I guessed it would be. He was a very big guy with a grim expression. I expected his tone to match his appearance. However, there was quite a contrast.

"Please tell me where I am?" My whisper matched his. We were alone in the entryway of the well-decorated home. Cameras were pointed at us.

"You are now property of the Mendez brothers; Santiago and Mauricio." He kneeled down to untie my restraints.

"What do you mean property?"

"It means you will remain here until they no longer have use for you." He stood.

"What kind of place is this?"

"This is a whorehouse that caters to the Mexican Cartel. The only way you will ever leave here is in a body bag." He never even blinked while breaking the disheartening news to me.

INDIA

Chapter Twenty-One
Nikki

While Mario and Junior were over to Ms. Claudia's for a visit, I was home catching up on cleaning and writing. The music on my iPod was bumping full blast, and a glass of Chardonnay rested next to my laptop. I rationalized that it was ok to have the wine because I was going to get an abortion anyway. I hadn't informed Mario yet. Actually, my plan was to get the abortion then tell him I had a miscarriage.

As K. Michelle blared through the sound system, I stroked the keypad with a vengeance. I was in the zone. My novel was only a few chapters short of being complete. Although Mario didn't fully agree with my decision to write an autobiography, he did understand it was my story, and I had every right to tell it. Anjela also thought I was wasting time. Still, she agreed to help me shop the manuscript to various publishing houses. I was determined to not permit their doubts to deter me from my objective nor take up space in my mind. The closer I got to completion, the more excited I became to get it published and into the hands of readers. The content was real and raw! I was convinced it would be well-received by the urban community.

After three hours of writing, I needed a break. I grabbed the wine bottle and slid it back into its hiding spot at the bottom of my closet. Next, I picked up my glass, taking it downstairs to wash it out. I couldn't run the risk of being found out by Mario. *DING. DONG.* The doorbell scared me so I jumped slightly. "Who is it?" I called out on my way to the door.

"It's Maine."

I shook my head as if I'd heard him wrong. What was this fool doing at my house, on my doorstep, like he belonged here?

"I think you should leave." I looked through the peephole. Sure as shit he was standing there dressed in an all black ensemble. His haircut was fresh, the gear was fresh, and he looked good. My heart fluttered and my palms were sweating. Not only hadn't I expected to see him again but I didn't anticipate having this type of reaction.

"We need to talk." He folded his arms as if he wasn't leaving until we talked. I sighed, opened the door, then stepped onto the porch. There was no way in hell I could allow him up in here and have Mario catch us. It was bad enough I was even entertaining this fool on the porch.

"What do you want?" I stood in front of the

door, watching up and down the street for Mario.

"I came to see you." He stepped closer to me. "I missed you."

"Maine, you ain't nothing but a liar. You used me to get your girl free. Now you have the audacity to stand here talking about you missed me? Nigga please!"

"I know what I did was fucked up and I apologize. I loved my girl and thought we could work but I realize we've grown apart."

"Isn't she pregnant?" I looked at him skeptically.

"We lost our son." He looked away briefly. "He was stillborn."

"Oh, I'm sorry to hear to that." Instinctively, I placed a hand on my stomach.

"It's okay. Everything happens for a reason you know." He responded, somewhat sad. "Me and my girl have been through a lot. This was the straw that finally broke the camel's back."

"It's not too late! You can still fix things." I felt bad for him.

"Our relationship is over. She's given up and I have too. Sometimes you have to recognize when it's over it's really over." The pain in his eyes was hard to ignore. He looked as if he needed a hug; I resisted the urge to do so. "Anyway, I came back here to see if you and I could start fresh."

"So you're jumping from one relationship into the next?"

"No, I'm not looking for a relationship. I just need a friend." His smile melted my heart like a bag of chocolate candy left out in the sun.

"Maine, how can we be friends? You lied to me and tried to kill my ex-husband?" It sounded silly to even be listening to this fool. However, I would be a liar if I didn't acknowledge I still felt something for him. Though it wasn't love, my attraction to him was undeniable.

"I can show you better than I can tell you. Let's start over and let nature take its course." He held out his hand for a truce.

"I'd like that." I placed my hand into his.

"Are you still writing that book of yours?" He leaned up against the banister.

"Actually, I'm almost done." It was refreshing to have someone genuinely take an interest in my book.

"That's good Nikki. Hopefully, I can get an advanced copy."

"Yeah right! You're not that interested in my life." I smiled coyly.

"You'd be surprised how interested I am in you." The tone of his voice put goose bumps on my neck.

"Maine, it was really nice seeing you but it's time for you to leave."

Confused, he said, "I thought we just made a truce."

"We did but Mario is staying with me for awhile. He'll be back here any minute."

"Can I at least call you sometimes?"

"Sure, I still have the same number." I was damn near pushing him off the porch.

"What about dinner?" He spoke on his way to the Aston Martin parked in my driveway. The very same Aston Martin we'd made love on when I got pregnant.

"Call me." My knees buckled as memories of that night invaded my mental space. Maine was a cold piece of work! Mario had better watch out.

INDIA

Chapter Twenty-Two
Gucci

I'd just pulled back up to the hotel and was retrieving bags from the trunk when my cell phone vibrated. "Shit!" I maneuvered a few bags in order to catch the call. "Hello."

"Hey baby, I'll be there in about an hour." Cartier and I had parted ways at the mall earlier. He had some business to handle. In view of that, we made a date to link up later for drinks and a movie. I was really excited to see him again and explore the new business venture.

"Ok, I'll be ready." I had already dropped Maria off on my way back to the hotel.

"Alright, I'll see you in a bit." He ended the call; I slid the phone into my bra, closing the trunk then headed inside. The doorman held the door open, I nodded my appreciation. As I bypassed the receptionist, she flagged me down.

"Ms., you have a visitor waiting over there for you." She pointed toward Mario and I almost wet my pants. He was pacing the floor with a menacing scowl. I wanted to tell homegirl to call security but played it cool.

Waltzing over to him with a frown of my own, I stopped directly in front of him. "What the fuck are you doing here?"

"Where the fuck is my fucking daughter?"

"She's spending the night out." There was no need to drop Satin's name. Mario would've surely gone over there and banged her door down.

"Bitch you better quit playing!" He stood, grabbing my face with such force he could've broken something.

"Let me go." I spoke as best I could through clinched teeth.

"Tell me where the fuck my daughter is!" His breathing was heavy.

"You will never see her again if you don't get your filthy paws off me."

"Sir, if you don't remove your hands from this lady, we will be forced to call the police," a security guard informed him as he approached us. Reluctantly, Mario released me, but not without a mush to the head first.

"Fuck you!" I hawked up a wad of spit and hurled it right into his face. If I had a strap on me, I would've put two bullets right between his eyes.

"Bitch!" He raised his hand to strike me but stopped. "This ain't over! You got until the end of the week to present my daughter." He warned on his way out of the building.

"Are you okay?" The security guard inquired.

"I'm fine."

Retreating upstairs to my hotel suite, a bitch was steaming mad! It took a shot of vodka and two blunts to calm my nerves. *How dare this nigga put his hands on me like some bitch in the streets?* I stepped from the shower and contemplated canceling my date with Cartier. I was in a funky mood and it wouldn't have been fair to him. Just as I picked up the phone, there was a knock on the door. My heart skipped three beats, fearful it was Mario back for more. Lightly, I crept to the door to see that it was Sam. "Damn!" I had forgotten to cancel our booty call. "Come on in." I opened the door.

"That's what the fuck I'm talking about right there." He looked my naked body over like it was a masterpiece.

"Whoa killa," I put my hand on his chest. "We can't do this today; I'm sorry."

"What?"

"I had a bad day and I ain't in the mood." That was the partial truth.

"Believe me, I can make your day much better." He whipped his penis out in one rapid motion.

"You know what Sam; I was thinking we shouldn't even be doing this. Mina is my girl and she's your fiancé. It's wrong." I retrieved the blue

Michael Kors dress, slipping it over my nakedness.

"You knew all that shit last week when you kept calling a nigga over here." He had an attitude. "Now you wanna have a heart–all of a sudden develop a conscience!"

"Look nigga, don't get beside yourself. You need to be grateful I even let you play in the pussy in the first place." I grabbed the freshly rolled blunt from my coffee table then lit it. Sam had my nerves on edge again. After lighting the medicinal cigarette, I tossed a hotel bath towel into the sink, wet it, and placed it under the door to prevent the smell from escaping the room.

"Can I get some head then? It's the least you could do since I drove all the way over here."

"Bye Sam." I pointed toward the door; he got the hint. On the way out, he tossed a few obscenities my way but fuck him.

Chapter Twenty-Three
Lovely

"Please help me!" I tried to head for the front door but the guard swooped me up in one motion.

"What's all the racket for?" A Caucasian woman approached the foyer wearing a sheer baby doll gown and four inch heels.

"Mauricio bagged another one. I was just about to bring her to you." The guard sat me back on the floor. "She's a feisty one."

"Let me go you clown." I tried shaking free–it was useless.

"We haven't had any black pussy since Carmen." The madam strutted down the marble stairs like America's Next Top Model. "What's your name girl?"

"Why?" I had no intentions on becoming chummy with her.

"Listen little winch!" She grabbed my face with a hand full of red nails. "You better learn some manners if you want to live to see tomorrow." She mushed my face away. I would've slugged this broad. Somehow, I knew her threats weren't idle. "Now I'm going to ask you one more time. What's your name girl?"

"Lovely."

"Well isn't that precious," she smirked. "From now on, you'll be addressed as number forty-two."

"Forty-two?" I repeated.

"Did I fucking stutter?" She looked as if she wanted to hit me. "Phillip take forty-two around back for branding."

"Branding?" I barely had time to speak the entire word before Phillip tossed me over his shoulder, carried me through the lavish home, then out back.

Once we were outside, he demanded that I remove my clothing, and toss everything into a garbage bag. While he plugged in an electric branding iron, I scoped the yard to see if I could break free. Not surprisingly, the place was swarming with security guards and secured by a barbed wire fence. "Lay down on your stomach!" He turned on the water hose.

"What?"

"Lay down now!" He hit me with the cold water. It stung so bad my skin felt as though I was being injected with several little needles. It didn't take long for me to get the hint. I had no idea what was about to happen next. Promptly, I dropped to the ground in order to stop the cold water assault. "Be still." He pulled out the electric branding iron then slapped it directly onto my right ass cheek.

"AHHH!" I screamed out in agony. The pain of being burnt with a blazing hot piece of iron was indescribable. The smell of blistering flesh, my flesh, was even worst.

After being branded with the number forty-two on my butt, I was taken back inside the house where the lingerie-wearing white lady waited for me. "Follow me." She headed up the back entrance of the home until we arrived on the second floor. "This is wear you'll sleep until I make room for you with the other whores." She pointed toward a door and waited for me to open it. It was the size of a coat closet. I turned to look at her, "I can barely fit in there."

"Forty-two please do as I instructed or face the consequences." Her expression was stone cold.

"Lady, I'm not sleeping in no fucking closet." Just as the last word left my tongue, I was hit with a volt of electricity from the pink taser gun in her hand. The voltage sent me flying into the small closet. I was unable to move and had peed on myself. The madam couldn't have given two shits about what she'd done. Furthermore, she calmly stepped back, closed the door, and locked it from the outside.

INDIA

Chapter Twenty-Four
Mina

I lay in bed just after midnight reading the newest novel entitled *Gangstress* by my favorite author when I heard Sam open the front door. I was about to pretend to be asleep but he was upstairs before I could even turn the lights off. "Hey." I nodded then placed the book on the nightstand.

"What's up." He removed his clothing.

"You left your phone at the hospital. I noticed you had a few missed calls and messages."

"Why are you going through my phone?" He glared at me.

"I didn't go through your phone. I was just making you aware." I was annoyed. If he was that concerned about the phone then he probably had something to hide. "You think you'd be grateful that you didn't lose the damn thing."

"Thank you for bringing the phone home baby," he stood. I thought he was about to take a shower but to my surprise he jumped in bed with me.

"What are you doing?"

"Let's make love." He bit on my nipples, then planted slow kisses from my navel down to my sweet spot. The shit was feeling too good.

Therefore, I basked in the moment. We hadn't been intimate in a while. In fact, when time permitted, I planned to hold a conversation about where our relationship was headed. For now, I just lay back and watched him work.

We made love for over an hour. I was impressed. He had skills originally but the passion he brought tonight had not been present in any of our previous sexual encounters. As we lay in the bed side by side trying to catch our breath, I looked into his eyes. Though he was with me physically, he wasn't present mentally. Something had been weighing heavily on his mind and I was tired of guessing. It was time to ask what was going on. "Sam, do you love me the way you did when you first came back?"

"Why do you ask that?" He looked at me. I didn't miss the fact that he answered my question with a question.

"As of late, your attitude has been shitty. You're rarely home. You haven't mentioned the wedding. And until tonight, we haven't made love in over a month." It felt good to get things off my chest.

"There are some things on my mind but they have nothing to do with you. So don't worry about it." He kissed my head.

"If something is bothering you, we should talk

about it. Maybe I can help?"

"Mina, I said it has nothing to do with you so let's drop it." He got up from the bed and headed for the shower.

The next day he was gone before seven in the morning. Our conversation or lack there of, left me confused. I needed to confide in a friend so I called Gucci to meet me for lunch. "Hey girl, what's up?" Gucci sashayed into the Bread Basket restaurant on Greenfield, north of Ten Mile Road. It had been awhile since we saw one another. I was so busy nursing baby Samantha back to health that my time was null in void. I missed her crazy self though.

"Hey mama!" I sprung up from the pleather seat with a smile. "Where is Maria?"

"She and Cartier are next door getting ice cream from Baskin-Robbins."

"He's back?"

"Yup!" She smiled.

"You know you're my girl but you're wrong for keeping Mario from his daughter. Yet, you're letting Cartier play daddy." I shook my head with a giggle.

"Mario can suck a fat one for all I care! In case you need to be reminded too, I run this shit! He'll see her on my terms!" She grabbed half of my corned beef sandwich and ate that shit like it was hers.

"You're cold girl," I laughed.

"That's my middle name," she laughed. "Enough about me, what's up with you?"

"I'm good, I guess." I shrugged. "I'm thinking about breaking up with Sam."

"What? Why?" She continued to eat my food.

"Ever since Chloe died, he's been acting all strange. We don't spend any time together and we barely talk anymore. If we do, he always finds a reason to get mad and leave. I was in a bad marriage for too long to deal with Sam and his bullshit. I can do bad all by myself."

"I feel that girl." She slapped me a high five. "But on a serious note you and Sam are cute together. He's dealing with a lot becoming a new father and all. Just give him time."

"How much time is the question? I feel like I've been patient long enough."

"I can't answer that for you Mina. Your heart will let you know," she winked.

"So are you and Cartier serious?" I reversed the attention back to her.

"I'm just taking it one day at a time with him."

"What are you gonna do about the marriage to Mario?"

"I'm going to get that shit annulled as soon as I

get time. Right now, I'm focused on building a new empire with Cartier."

"So you're leaving the H.O.F. organization?" The acronym was tatted on her neck. I couldn't believe she was done with it so suddenly.

"Yeah." She looked sad. "Me and Mario will never be what we used to be. And that's not good for business. It's time to move on ya know."

"Damn!" I was sad. Although the organization meant nothing to me, I knew what it meant to her. It was her baby and she was letting it go.

"It's okay. Please believe I will definitely land on top."

"I know you will, you always do."

"The thought of starting over is scary but I plan to take a few of my workers with me." She finished up the last of my sandwich.

"This will probably initiate a war between you and Mario. You know that right?"

"I ain't got nothing left for him Mina. Right now, he's public enemy number one!" She was dead serious.

"Do you don't think your friendship will ever be salvageable?" The two of them had been best friends since they were sixteen.

"I don't need no backstabbing friends," she declared.

"He's having a party on Saturday. You should come and bring the baby." I tried to lighten the mood.

"Bitch please!" She laughed. "If I come through there, it'll be to blow his head off."

"I could take Maria if you want." I glanced pass Gucci to see Cartier who had just walked in.

"Girl, haven't you been listening? He will see her on my time."

"Hey baby." Cartier handed Maria to her mom then took a seat.

"You remember my friend Mina don't you?" Gucci introduced us.

"What's good ma." He nodded at me then looked back at Gucci. "You ready?"

"It's time to go already?" Gucci glanced down at her watch. "Mina, we have a meeting to attend. It was good to catch up though. Call me later and we'll set another date."

"Put this on the bill." Cartier slapped a fifty dollar bill on the table.

"See ya later." I watched the couple leave the restaurant and couldn't help but wonder why I felt uneasy about the new man in her life.

Chapter Twenty-Five
Lovely

Sometime the next day I was released from the closet by the madam, who made no apologies for what she had done. I could tell she was a smug bitch and couldn't wait to get in that ass. "Follow me!" She walked with her nose in the air up the grand staircase. I followed her down the long hallway to the last door on the left. The room filled with women became silent once I arrived. Because she was the head bitch in charge around here, everyone appeared to be frightened of the white woman. "This is your bunk." She gestured toward the bottom bunk near the door. It was already made up with white sheets and a tan blanket. The room was large and resembled a boot camp facility with several bunk beds strategically placed throughout.

"Do I get my clothes back?" It was a dumb question because like me, all the other girls were butt naked.

"Dinner is in an hour." She snobbishly turned around then headed out the door.

Once she was out of earshot, the chatter amongst the other women resumed. It wasn't long before one of them introduced herself. "Hi, I'm

Daphnie." The young white girl smiled.

"What's up." I nodded.

"Aren't you going to tell me your name?" She made herself comfortable on my bed. I didn't like the fact that her bare coochie was on my bed but I didn't make any beef about it.

"No offense Daphnie but I'm not in the mood to be social."

"I didn't mean anything by it. It just helps to pass the time away," she confessed.

"How did you end up here?" I looked her over from head to toe. Her face was youthful but her body looked worn out. Her breasts looked as if they had been sucked on one two many times and her vagina needed a face-lift. I'd never seen someone's clitoris hanging beyond their vaginal lips.

"I was a working girl looking for some quick cash. Mauricio pulled up in an expensive car and offered top dollar for my services. Of course, I jumped into his ride with no hesitation." She looked down at the floor. "He said he was taking me back to his house instead he brought me here."

"How long have you been here?"

"I don't know exactly; I ain't seen a calendar in forever." She smiled with buck teeth. "However, the day I came here was October tenth, the day before my son's birthday."

"That was almost ten months ago." I shook my head in disbelief.

"I think about that day every time I close my eyes." She chewed on her bottom lip. "I wasn't even supposed to be working that day. However, I wanted to buy something special for my boy and needed a little more money."

"That shit is deep."

"So what's your story?" She lay back and made herself comfortable. Because she had just spilled her guts to me, I decided to spill mine to her.

"I left the house yesterday evening with plans to commit suicide." The expression on her face was disbelief. "I headed to the bar for a drink to calm my nerves. Mauricio had the bartender to spike it."

"Maybe it's a blessing you ended up here." Her green eyes peered into mine.

"I don't see how being kidnapped is a blessing." This girl was delusional.

"Well had you not ended up here, you would've been dead by now."

"This shit ain't no better than death!" I replied angrily.

"It's not that bad. They feed us, they put a roof over our heads, and they let us live as long as we obey the rules." She was about as dumb as a box of rocks.

"Girl, this ain't no way to treat people. Are you crazy?"

"Where I came from, I was barely making ends meet. I was on drugs and my son suffered because of it. This may sound ridiculous but in a way they saved my life."

"That does sound ridiculous especially because you're never gonna get outta here." I rolled my eyes. "Anyway, what actually happens around here?"

"It's basically a high-end brothel." She informed me. "The brothers exclusively cater to the mob. They host parties every other night. We walk the room and mingle. Eventually, someone will pay for sex with you. If you're lucky, one of them will buy you indefinitely." She stood from the bed.

"What does that mean?" I didn't like the sound of that.

"It means they purchase you, and take you with them."

"Like slavery?" I frowned.

"Yup." She replied. "You become the property of whoever purchases you.

Chapter Twenty-Six
Gucci

After dropping Maria off to Satin, Cartier and I headed to see our potential connect. His name was Bayani. He was straight from the Philippines. Up until recently, I had no idea there was even a drug cartel in their country. Initially, Mario was the one who put me on game. He claimed Bayani was looking to expand his family business to the United States. He wanted to flood the black market with one hundred percent, authentic, raw white powder and put Columbia and Mexico out of business. In order to do so, he decided to solicit the assistance of Detroit, Miami and New York. Flying state to state, he met with the highest selling organizations in each city to determine who he wanted to do business with. Luckily, we had no competition in Detroit during that time. I hoped he wouldn't be upset when he noticed Mario was not in attendance.

"Is this the place?" Cartier looked at me while I looked at the GPS. We were given an address and a time to be there. It was way out in the boondocks at a warehouse.

"Let's get out and see." I left my purse in the car because my gun was inside of it. I figured

Bayani more than likely had a ton of security just waiting for a reason to pop a cap in my ass. I didn't want to alarm them with my piece.

"Right this way." A man in a black suit escorted us toward the door.

Once inside, we had to go through a metal detector and be frisked before meeting with Bayani.

"This is not Mario Wallace!" His voiced elevated two levels, which caused our security escort to draw his weapon.

"I can explain!" I raised my hands. "This is Cartier Jones and he's with me."

"Where is Mario Wallace?" Bayani frowned.

"He had an accident." Thinking fast, I used Mario's gunshot wound as a quick cover. "He was shot in the head a few weeks ago and is recovering."

"I don't like surprises. You should've come alone." Bayani's tone was now calm. He told the guard to leave then showed us to the boardroom table in the middle of the wide open space.

"My apologies Bayani. It won't happen again.

"It better not." He threatened before getting down to business.

The entire meeting lasted only forty minutes but we covered a lot during that time. He was very thorough and meticulous, not leaving out one single detail. His family owned a casket business which they used as a front to smuggle dope into the Unites States. "Everything will ship on the first of every month. The product will be in the lining of caskets."

"I can't wait to get started." I stood from the table.

"One last thing, Gucci." He smiled. "May I have a word in private."

"Okay." I looked back at Cartier who nodded.

"My organization is tight-knit. It has never been infiltrated because we've stuck to our own kind. My family was hesitant about this business enterprise. However, I assured them they had nothing to fear. I promised I would handpick each individual and I have except for your friend here." He stared at Cartier. "Since you brought him into my circle, you're responsible for his actions."

"I give you my word; Cartier is a stand-up guy."

"Where I come from, your word is all you have and your life depends on it." The subtle message was not lost on me as I read between the lines. Basically, I was being warned. If Cartier didn't prove to be who I said he was, then it would be the death of me.

Chapter Twenty-Seven
Nikki

All week I had been on pins and needles thinking Maine would call or show up again when Mario was around. Thank goodness he hadn't. Mario had been in a sour mood ever since his run in with Gucci. He told me he almost laid fists on her but had to catch himself. She was the mother of his child. For that reason, he still had to respect her. I was proud he hadn't let his anger get the best of him. Nevertheless, she was playing with fire. One of these days, he would leave home without any manners and it would be lights out for her.

On the way to Mario's birthday party at the Moet Lounge on Woodward, I noticed he was eerily silent. "What's wrong with you?"

"Something ain't right. I feel it." His leg bounced up and down uncontrollably.

"What do you mean something ain't right?" Subconsciously, I peeped the scene to spot any potential dangers lurking.

"I can't explain it. I haven't been able to hold a civil conversation with Gucci. I haven't been out on the streets like I need to. I feel like I'm losing touch with what's going on around me."

"Rio you need to let them streets go anyway."

Hitting the blinker, I switched to the right lane.

"I am Nikki, but first I gotta tie up a few loose ends."

"You keep on saying that–fuck those loose ends!" It was frustrating that he couldn't leave the streets alone. How many more bad things had to happen to us before he would wise up? The sound of his phone interrupted us.

"Speak on it." The call sounded over the car's speakers. Mario's phone was connected to the Bluetooth system.

"Yo boss, it's dry out here." Someone spoke.

"What you fucking mean it's dry?" Mario sat up in his seat.

"We ain't got no product. I spoke wit' O. He said he been blowing up Gucci for the re-up but she ain't answering.

"So y'all been without work all this time?" Mario was fuming.

"Yup!"

"Let me make some calls; I'll hit you back." He ended the call then proceeded to make a new one.

"What up boss." Omar answered in his usual slow, southern drawl. He was from Georgia.

"O, what the fuck is going on bruh?"

"Man yo gurl done played us." His pronunciation of the word "girl" always made me laugh. "She took the money on the second and got ghost. I been callin' her 'bout the re-up but she ain't answerin'. I would've been called you but I thought she was gon' come through. Then I heard we being phased out. Niggas on the block getting antsy and shit."

"Fuck you mean, we being phased out?"

"Word on the streets is a few days ago there was some new nigga on the scene with that killa for the low low."

"How low?" Mario frowned.

I wasn't really into his street dealings but I knew enough about the H.O.F. organization to know that for years Mario had the lowest prices.

"This new nigga is runnin' bogo sales my dog." The caller spoke louder.

"What the fuck is bogo?" Mario rested his back up against the seat.

"Buy one get one free." Omar replied.

"Are you serious right now?"

"Blood, I'm serious as a heart attack. I didn't wanna tell you this but these new niggas done already shut down the spots on Piedmont, East Outer Drive, and Flanders."

"Who is these niggas?" Mario sat up in the seat.

"Word roun' the way is it's Gucci and her new

ol' man." Omar sounded like he regretted being the bearer of bad news. "They done recruited half of the squad already. When niggas found out they was gettin' money, they jumped ship."

"That bitch!" He barked. "O, let me hit you back."

"Fa sho."

"She did this." Mario bellowed.

"Did what?" I questioned.

"Before I got shot, there was a deal on the table with my Filipino connect. Gucci knew about it and the bitch did the deal for that nigga she fuckin'!"

"Baby, calm down." I didn't want his blood pressure to shoot up.

"Do you know how much money I just lost? And now this bitch is puttin' my crew out of business." He hit the dashboard.

"Maybe it's a good thing." I whispered; Mario looked at me sideways. "All I'm saying Mario is this is your opportunity to leave the game. Wash your hands of that life and start over. It's not like you're broke.

"Fuck that! She crossed the line!" He spat. "I should kill that bitch!"

Chapter Twenty-Eight
Gucci

"I'ma be fresh as hell if the feds watching…I'ma be fresh as hell if the feds watching…" The sound of my cell phone startled me awake. "Hello!" I answered with an attitude. First of all, I wasn't ready to wake up. Secondly, I didn't recognize the phone number.

"It's almost eleven o'clock! What the fuck you still doing sleep?" Cartier sounded like he'd been up for hours.

"What the fuck are you doing up?" I rolled my eyes.

"Money never sleeps baby girl." I heard him flick the lighter in the background. He was probably lighting a blunt. Cartier loved to wake and bake. "Get dressed and meet me down in the lobby in twenty minutes."

"Boy, the only thing I'll be doing in twenty minutes is sleeping." I looked over at Maria who was knocked out with a pacifier hanging off the tip of her lips. After my run-in with Mario and taking the deal with Bayani, it was imperative I move to another hotel. The only person who knew I was here is Cartier.

"Come on, I want to take you somewhere!" He pleaded.

"Cartier, you've been taking me somewhere everyday for a week now. I appreciate all the generosity but I'm sleepy," I whined. He had already taken Maria and I shopping, to breakfast, lunch, dinner, and to the zoo. I didn't want to sound ungrateful but there was nowhere else for us to go.

"Girl, turn those sheets loose. You can sleep when you die! I'll give you thirty minutes. If you ain't down here by then, I guess I'll just have to call the realtor back and decline…"

"Why didn't you say you were taking me to see a house?" My ass was out of bed with the quickness. "See you in thirty." I hung up and headed to the closet. The small space was filled with all of the brand new things Cartier had purchased for me this week. He told me to trash everything Mario had bought and I did just that. It nearly broke my heart to dump everything, including my jewelry. However, I wanted to rid myself of anything that reminded me of his bitch ass.

Removing the tag from a blue pair of spandex jeans, I slid them up my bare ass. Wearing panties was for the birds! I needed my coochie to be free. Furthermore, there was nothing worse than those damn panty lines to kill an outfit. I slipped on a bra and white t-shirt, then my gold necklace. It read: *Trust no nigga.* I pulled my Pilipino weave back into a ponytail and slipped on a Detroit Tigers snapback cap. When I went to retrieve the blue and orange Nikes from the closet, I noticed Maria was waking up. "Hey there pretty girl." I planted kisses on her pie face while she giggled. Her curly hair was all over the place but it was nothing a brush and bow-bows couldn't fix. "Let's get you dressed little mama." Grabbing one of the OshKosh hangers from the closet, I put Maria on a pink onesie with a white ruffled skirt. I rubbed her down with baby lotion then slipped on her pink booties. We were almost ready to go, I just needed to grab my purse, the diaper bag, and place Maria in her car seat/stroller contraption. BUZZ. BUZZ. I grabbed the cell phone and read a message from Sam: What's up?

I wasn't in the mood to text so I called him. "Hey Gucci."

"What Sam, I'm busy!" I rolled my eyes.

"I'm trying to slide though and see what's up between those butterscotch legs of yours."

"Nigga, didn't I tell you I was done fucking with you."

"What if I ain't done fucking with you." His voice was more serious now.

"Is that a threat?"

"I'm not a plaything. You don't decide when we're done."

He hung up on me and not a moment too soon. I was just about to hang up on him. Niggas was always catching feelings and getting the game twisted. I needed to keep him away from me so I sent a text: It's best you go back to work for Mario. I no longer need you on my team. After minutes without a reply, I placed the phone into my pocket then went back to doing me.

As I pushed the stroller pass the mirror, I smiled. Never had I imagined this life for myself. I was always used to living in the fast lane but I was digging this mommy thing.

"I'ma be fresh as hell if the feds watching…I'ma be fresh as hell if the feds watching."

"Cartier, I'm coming." It never occurred to me to check the caller ID.

"It's Mario!" The tone he used signified he was pissed. He probably thought I called him by the wrong name on purpose.

"Oh."

"That's all you gon' say?"

"What do you want me to say?" I smacked my lips, pushing the stroller out of the room.

"You know why the fuck I'm calling!" He

snapped. "We need to meet pronto!"

"We ain't got shit to talk about."

"So you just gonna take the deal with the Pilipino like that?"

"Straight like that." The coldness in my tone was like a machete to Mario's flesh.

"I don't know what hurts more, the fact that you played me on the connect or that you stole nigga's from my organization."

"Mario let's not talk about what hurts because I guarantee you'll lose this round." The nerve of this nigga to be acting like he was oblivious to shit he put me through.

"Fuck outta here Gucci!" He yelled. "You acting like I was the only one fuckin' around. Didn't you fuck your mans in my crib? Let's not forget the facts baby girl."

"Look, I gotta go." Hanging up in his face gave me brief satisfaction. I wanted to do some volatile shit to him but handcuffs didn't look good on me.

"I'ma be fresh as hell if the feds watching…I'ma be fresh as hell if the feds watching." I knew it was Mario again so I turned the phone off. He was not gonna ruin my day with his bullshit.

Stepping from the elevator, my eyes landed on the finest brown skinned nigga this side of Michigan. Cartier sat on the arm of the couch in the lobby talking on his cell phone. As I made my way over to him, I took in the red Cole Haan loafers, black Dickies, and a red button-down. The red and black Detroit hat put a smile on my face. I guess it's true, great minds do think alike. "Pimp, let me call you back, my girl just got down here." He slid the phone into the back pocket of his pants then stood to greet me. "What's up sexy?"

"Nothing much." I smiled for no reason at all. Cartier just did that to me. It was something about his swag, his boss-like attitude, and the expensive cologne that had me wet with anticipation of our next romp in the bedroom. The man was definitely gifted between the legs. He put it down like no lover I had ever been with.

"Can a nigga get a hug or something?" He stretched his long arms open wide and I dove in. Cartier was a safe place for me. He was my first love and my first sexual partner. Had he not been locked up for so long, my life would've turned out much differently. No doubt ya girl would've still been a hustler's wife but I never would've met Mario or had Maria.

"So where are we going?" I quizzed.

"You'll see." He kneeled down to kiss Maria's forehead. "Now come on and no more questions."

Chapter Twenty-Nine
Mina

"Where are my keys?" Sam yelled from the foyer. I was coming up from the basement with laundry.

"Why are you yelling?" His attitude lately was unnerving.

"Because I'm looking for my keys and you were the last one with them." He lashed out. "You took my car to show a house yesterday, remember? I told you to leave the keys right here at the front door but you don't listen."

"Sam don't speak to me like a fucking kid!"

"Anyway, where the hell are my keys?" His stare mimicked mine.

"When I came home yesterday I placed the keys right where you told me to. Then you made a run after that - remember? I found the keys in a pair of your jeans I just took to wash." I retrieved the keys from the laundry hamper, tossing them at him." The look on his face was priceless.

"My bad." His apology lacked emotion. "I'm going to holla at Mario. I'll be back in a few."

"I thought you said we were gonna lie in bed and watch movies?" All week long we were constantly on the go, ripping, and running. We were barely able to spend time together.

"Not today, I got business to handle."

"What the hell is wrong with you? You've been acting strange and I don't like it at all." It was time to put my foot down. The tension between us was too thick.

"Ain't nothing up Mina," he sighed. "I'm going to handle some business. I'll try to make it fast a'ight?"

"Since when did you rejoin the drug game?" The more time he spent with Mario, the less time he spent with me. I knew he was back in the game but hadn't said anything.

"Some shit came up," was all he said on his way out the door.

I stood there in shock long enough to hear the engine on his car crank up then pull out of the driveway. "Ain't this a bitch!" Resisting the urge to grab the cordless and blow his phone up wasn't easy. However, I did call Gucci. "Mina you won't believe this!" She squealed. "Cartier just bought me a mansion!"

"Oh my god, are you serious!?"

"Girl yes, you have to come and check it out." She went on and on. I didn't want to put a damper on her day. For that reason, I chose not to tell her why I had called.

"Ok girl, I will. You go ahead and celebrate; I'll get with you later." I ended the call and headed up to my bedroom. I remember when Sam purchased this home for us and the family we wanted to have. Seemingly, my fairytale was taking a turn for the worse. I loved Sam and wanted to fight for us. In contrast, it was hard to fight when I didn't know why we were fighting in the first place.

Once upstairs, I dropped the laundry basket onto the bed. I began folding the clothes, stopping midway. Suddenly, I had the urge to go out and listen to music. It was still early, I wanted to be in the company of people in good spirits. Grabbing a pink, scoop neck dress with the back out and a pair of wedges, I quickly slipped them on. My hair was already done. I wasn't into makeup. Therefore, a little dab of CHANEL N°5 behind the ears and I was ready. When I reached the main floor, I gave myself the once-over in the mirror, then grabbed my purse. I armed the alarm and stepped onto the porch. "Where are you going?" Sam stood there with a smirk.

"I thought you were gone? What happened?" Although startled by his presence, I was happy to see him.

"I came back to apologize for my behavior. There's just been a lot of shit on my mind and I'm stressed."

"What's wrong baby? Can I help?" I stepped into his space, embracing him in a hug.

"There are a few things I have to tell you but not today." He shook his head. "Since you're all dressed up, I'm gonna take you out and make up for lost time."

"Sam, I would much rather know what's going on with you."

"Not right now ma. Let's just enjoy the moment." He leaned down and kissed the side of my neck sending shivers down my body.

An hour later, we were seated inside the VIP area in Club Plush. It was the hottest club in Novi that catered to the after work crowd. All the drinks and food were half off. Party hours were from four to nine. It turned into a regular club after that. Demographics for the average partygoer were a mixture of African Americans and Caucasians, ranging between twenty-five and thirty-five in age. Sam wasn't much of a club dude but he obliged my request to hear some good music.

Currently, they were playing the new Miley Cyrus joint, all the white girls were twerking, or so they thought. "You want a drink?" He leaned in close to my ear.

"Yeah, I'll take a sex on the beach."

"Girl, we can head to the beach right now." He winked then waved the waiter over. While they conversed, the DJ switched gears, playing hip hop. Two Chainz and Drake were now blaring throughout the room. I was up on my feet, headed to the dance floor. It felt good to move and be free. I hadn't been out in a while and was having so much fun. A few younger men even tried to dance with me, which boosted my ego. It was good to know a girl still had it.

On my way back to the table, a woman wearing a fierce Donna Karan mini dressed bumped into me, causing her drink to spill down the front of my outfit. I would've brushed the shit off but homegirl didn't even attempt to apologize. She kept walking with her friend like nothing happened. *Oh hell no!* I followed them then tapped her on the shoulder. "What!?" She turned around with major attitude.

"You spilled your drink on my dress. The least you could've done was apologize." This young girl was going to learn the importance of manners if I had anything to do about it.

"Bitch, don't nobody give a fuck about that dress you found on the Walmart clearance rack," she laughed. It was my desire to inform her this was no Walmart special but it wasn't important.

"Mina, what's going on?" Sam approached me with a bottle of Heineken in one hand and my sex on the beach in another.

"Not now baby." Without hesitation, I grabbed the bottle from him and doused her with the beer.

"You bitch!" She screamed as she lunged at me. Quickly stepping aside, I watched her fly into a couple dancing behind me. Now I was the one laughing, until her friend began to speak.

"Sam? What are you doing here?"

"Tynika?" He looked as if he had just seen a ghost.

"How do you two know each other?" I crossed my arms, waiting for Sam to form a sentence.

"I'm his baby's mama." She extended a manicured hand.

"What?" I shrieked.

"Mina, that's what I wanted to talk to you about." He attempted to clarify.

"You must be the woman he left me and his son for." She spoke over the music.

"His son?" I was stunned and hurt beyond belief.

The entire ride home was silent. I couldn't believe this nigga had a son and didn't think enough of me to share that information. "Mina, I know you're mad but I can explain."

"I'm listening."

"I met Tynika while I was dating Chloe. We messed around and I got her pregnant. I didn't even know about the baby until after I proposed to you. I was going to tell you but the timing was off. You were already being a good sport about baby Samantha."

"How old is the kid?"

"He's one."

"What's his name?" I sighed, relaxing my shoulders. There was no reason to be mad for real. I mean the baby was conceived before he and I were an item. Despite that, my spirit was broken. I wanted desperately to have a baby with him but now he has two.

"Solomon." His voice was low like he was ashamed of the fact he had brought two babies into this relationship.

"You should've told me Sam." I shook my head.

"I know Mina but I also realized the news would hurt you."

"Well it hurts worst to find out by some random bitch in the club."

"Baby, I'm sorry." He pulled into the driveway, turning the engine off. "You've been asking what's wrong with me, now you have it. I was just so afraid of losing you.

"Sam, for several months I've been feeling pushed away. If you're trying to keep me, you have a mighty funny way of showing it."

"I know. I know." He grasped my face. "I promise on my life, I'll do any and everything I can to make it up to you."

"No more secrets right?" My heart couldn't take anything else.

"No more secrets." Sam smiled.

Chapter Thirty
Lovely

Tonight was the first party I would be attending. I was nervous yet curious about the goings on around here. Sometime after nightfall I could hear guests arriving, as well as the sound of music. It seemed to be a mixture of opera over a Mexican beat. I wanted to peak out the door but it was locked. "The madam should be here soon." Daphnie announced seconds before the door opened.

"Okay ladies, It's Show Time!" She clapped her hands while everyone stood at attention. Assembled at the door, was a single file line. No one made a sound. "Remember to be on your best behavior." Prior to leading us away from the room and down the staircase, she looked directly at me.

Moments later, we entered a large room. Men lounged around in smoking jackets puffing cigars and sipping on cocktails. At first, it was embarrassing to walk around a room full of strangers in my birthday suit. I felt like everyone was looking at the number burned unto my ass. "Varmos a bailar." The salt and pepper haired gentleman to my right held out his hand. The dude was clean from head to toe, dressed in Gianni

Versace. Two diamond rings rested on his wedding and pinky fingers. His shirt was unbuttoned to reveal a mass of chest hair. Although he spoke Spanish, he appeared to be Italian to me.

"Huh?" I didn't know what the hell he was saying.

"Let's dance." His hand was still out waiting for me to take it. I wanted to tell him this wasn't my kind of music but I could feel eyes gawking in our direction.

"What the hell, let's do it." I placed my hand into his and prepared to tango or some shit but he had other plans.

"My dear, I don't mean dance on the dance floor. I want to take the party to the bedroom," he smiled.

"Ok." I smiled nervously as he escorted me pass the other guests and out of the room.

Once inside one of the bedrooms on the main floor, he stood there. "I want you to undress the King."

"No problem King." Slowly, I undid the last two buttons on his shirt then made my way to his silk pants. They were pressed to death; the creases were so crisp, I almost cut myself.

"While you're down there, you might as well suck on the prince." He referred to his manhood. I was ready to throw up! Seriously, giving up some pussy was one thing but putting a stranger's dick in my mouth was a whole other situation. Nonetheless, I swallowed hard, closed my eyes, and slid the shriveled up piece of flesh into my mouth. I don't know what I expected it to taste like, but it wasn't as bad as I thought.

Slowly, I bobbed my head back and forth until his erection was at its maximum length. "Yeah, that's it." He moaned. When I was finished, I stood from the floor then headed over to the bed. King or whatever his name was took no time grabbing a condom from the nightstand then diving deep inside the walls of my body. His rhythm was off; he didn't quite hit the spot but it wasn't the worst. In fact, I was glad my first time was with him. From the looks of some of those other cats, I had snagged the best one. *Knock. Knock.*

"Hurry up in there." Someone spoke into the door. "I just paid for a round with her."

"I'm after you." Another person added.

"Looks like you'll be a busy girl tonight." King was smiling but I wanted to cry. At this rate, my coochie would be looking like Daphnie's in no time.

INDIA

Chapter Thirty-One
Nikki

"Are you ready?" The nurse smiled. She was a skinny woman with brunette hair, wearing a black scrub top and matching bottoms. I was at the abortion clinic with Anjela. Today was the day–I was nervous. Mario was out in the streets and Junior was with his grandmother.

"Are you sure you want to do this cuz?" Anj looked up from the file she was reading.

"I'm sure." I grabbed my purse, following the nurse.

"Do you want me come with you?"

"No, I'm good." I headed down the hallway. She checked my weight first, then my blood pressure, and finally, my temperature. While she notated the necessary information on my chart, I couldn't help but stare at the women coming and going to and from each room. The youngest girl I saw was accompanied by her mother. She looked to be no more than fifteen. The next woman I saw was accompanied by her husband I presume. I'd overheard them talking about not being able to feed another mouth; and this was the best choice for their family.

Once inside the room, I was handed a hospital

gown and told to wait for the doctor. As I undressed, a feeling of uneasiness came over me. I wasn't sure if this was the right thing to do. I lie back on the table, placing a hand to my stomach. The baby was too small to kick but just knowing it was alive moved me. There was no way I could go through with this. Just as the door opened, I sat up abruptly. "Hello Ms. Wallace. My name is Dorian." The doctor entered the room in full surgical gear.

"Doctor, I'm sorry but I've changed my mind." The tears were flowing uncontrollably.

"Would you like to see a counselor?" He handed me the Kleenex box from the counter.

"No, I just need to leave."

"I understand Ms. Wallace." He nodded before leaving the room quietly. Jumping up from the table, I slid on my shit. I never wanted to step foot back in a place like this again. Who cares who my baby's father is? All that matters is my child is loved.

"Anj let's go." I hurried through the office like a tropical breeze.

"What's wrong?" She inquired, as she gathered her work in a rush. People were looking at me sideways but I didn't give a damn. Once outside, I took a profound breath. Just minutes ago, I almost killed a precious gift given to me by God. I definitely didn't judge anyone for their choices but abortion wasn't for me. "Slow down!" Anjela yelled.

"I'm sorry cuz; I just had to get up outta there."

"I feel you." She stuffed the papers into her briefcase. "I take it you're going to keep the baby then right?"

"Yes, I'm going to keep it." Wrapping my arms around myself I wanted to scream from the rooftop that I was keeping my child.

"Good," she smiled. "Does Mario want another son or another daughter?"

"I don't know." I responded on the way to her car.

"What's wrong? You sound sad. Don't tell me you're second guessing your decision."

"It's not that." I sighed, sliding into the passenger seat.

"Then what in the hell is it?" She cranked up the vehicle.

"Maine came to see me the other day."

"What!?" She screamed. "What did he say?"

"For starters, he apologized. Then he said he wanted to be friends and start fresh."

"How do you feel about that, seeing as how you're trying to work things out with Mario?"

"Honestly, I love Mario but he loves the streets.

I'm not about that life anymore. Maine is more refined. I feel like he and I are on the same page when it comes to life." I never thought I'd ever choose any man over Mario but Maine gave me things to think about.

"What do you plan to do?"

"There's nothing wrong with having a friend, right?" I giggled.

"Your ass won't be laughing when Mario finds out." Anjela shook her head, putting the car in gear.

Chapter Thirty-Two
Gucci

When Cartier said we were going to look at houses, I had no idea what was in store. Unbeknownst to me, he had already purchased a 10,000 square foot lavish home. "What in the world is going on?" I asked as we pulled into the circular driveway. There were several people outside in various uniforms waving at us.

"Welcome home baby." Cartier parked the car next to a black and chrome 2014 G550 G-Wagon by Mercedes Benz. Both the whip and the house were covered in large pink bows.

"Are you kidding me?" I punched him on the arm and jumped out of the car like it was on fire. "This is ours?"

"Yup." He retrieved Maria from the car seat and carried her while I took in the magnificent scenery. "I call it the luxury estate baby."

"This place is gorgeous!" I squealed. "I can't wait for Satin and Mina to see it."

"Come over here for a second and meet the staff."

"The staff?" I smiled. Living in the lap of luxury wasn't something new for me but never had I been equipped with staff.

"This is Roseanne the housekeeper."

"Buenos dias senorita." She did a curtsy. I didn't know what to say or do so I curtsied back.

"This is Walter the resident chef."

"Morning ma'am. I specialize is gourmet cuisine from all over the world. You name it and I'll make it."

"Resident as in he will live here too?" I looked from Walter to Cartier.

"Yes. There are separate living quarters toward the back of the property line for Walter and Sophia."

"Okay, well nice to meet you Walter." I smiled at the middle-aged, balding gentleman in blue jeans and a chef's coat.

"Last but not least, this is Sophia, Maria's new nanny." She was a middle-aged, pleasantly plump, Pilipino woman with black hair and grey temples.

"Nice to meet you Ms." She smiled and instinctively reached for Maria. I thought she would begin to cry in the arms of the unfamiliar pale woman. To my astonishment, Maria said nothing. Furthermore, she lay on the stranger's shoulder like she didn't have a care in the world.

"Come on baby let me show you the rest of the crib." Cartier pulled me pass the staff and into the massive house.

There were gold columns, oversized windows with panoramic views, and each room had already been decorated impeccably. More often than not, I would've pitched a bitch about not contributing to the design process. Yet, this place was beautiful! There was a formal living and dining area, chef's kitchen, a great room, seven bedrooms, and eight bathrooms. The bonus was the movie theater and two lane bowling alley in the basement. To date, I had only seen this shit on MTV's show *Cribs*. "Do you like it?"

"Of course I do!" I beamed with excitement.

"To be honest, I was already having this shit built before I returned to Detroit." Cartier took a seat on the spiral staircase.

"Why in the world would you want to live in a big ass place like this?" I took a seat on the step between his legs.

"This might sound corny but I knew I would find you and we'd start a family here. At the time, I wasn't aware you had already started a family without me."

"I didn't think you were ever getting out of prison." For some odd reason, I felt the need to explain.

"Yeah, I know." He tugged on my hair playfully. "I hate to sound like an ass but I'm glad you and homeboy didn't work out."

"We were never truly meant to be, I realize that now." In essence, it hurt to face the truth. Then again, it was what it was. Just because two people love one another doesn't necessarily equate to them being destined to be together.

"Good! Because if you fuck around and go back to that nigga, me and you will have some problems."

"Boy stop! Mario is the furthest thing from my mind." That was the truth so help me God.

"What about Maria?"

"What about her?" I turned to face him. "I'll continue to raise her. And when I'm ready for him to see her, we'll make arrangements."

"Gucci, you can't hold her hostage." He laughed. "That's his daughter too."

"Whose side are you on?" The last time Cartier and Mario were in the same place, they fought. Now he's defending his enemy.

"Baby, you never have to question my loyalty. I'm just keeping it one hundred. That's her father, and every little girl needs their daddy. You see how those ratchet bitches on television turned out."

"Are you saying you don't want the responsibility of being in her life?" I snapped, already realizing why. He was telling the truth but I didn't want to hear it. I was furious with Mario. Cartier wants me to do the right thing too. Nevertheless, I wasn't feeling it.

"You think I would've moved y'all in here if I didn't want the responsibility of being in her life!?" His voice rose. "Needless to say, I would like to be her father, but I'm not so I respect that."

"The Cartier I know would've said to hell with that nigga!" I laughed. "When did you become so wise?"

"Age will do that to you. Just keep on living." He said it like he was light-years older than me instead of four. "But on a serious note, as long as Mario don't cross you or Maria, we're good."

INDIA

Chapter Thirty-Three
Lovely

I'd be lying if I said being in this hellhole had gotten better with time. I'd been fucked by more men than I cared to remember. Some of them were old as dirt with wrinkled penis's and sagging balls. They could barely get it up. Still, they wanted me to do all kinds of freaky shit. I was sick to my stomach. Even so, I learned to never complain and pretended to enjoy it. I didn't want to be killed.

This week alone, I witnessed two women lose their lives simply for giving bad blowjobs. "Number forty-two snap out of it!" The madam snapped her fingers. I'd come to learn that her name is Lucy. After successfully running a prostitution ring in California, she was hired by the brothers. Her clients included tons of A-list celebrities. She's been in the industry for over ten years. Her business was shut down when the feds caught on and hit her with charges. They wanted her to give up her clientele in exchange for freedom but she was no snitch! Homegirl did a five year bid and never looked back. "Forty-two, did you hear me? I said It's Show Time." This time, she pulled the parlor doors open to reveal a room full of men in casual attire. As usual, the place was smoky and reeked of Tequila.

There were twelve women on tonight's shift, twenty of us in total. While we walked around the room in birthday suits, the other eight women stood around in lingerie holding trays and pouring drinks. Because of their menstrual cycle, they were given the night off. *Lucky bitches!*

I sauntered around the room barefoot, making eye contact with no one except Mauricio. Every time he looked at me, I wanted him to remember what he did to me. I wanted him to know that I hadn't forgotten. If my eyes were daggers, he would've died a thousand times already. "Forty-Two. I want forty-two."

I turned to see an older, Hispanic man dressed in tan trousers and a striped shirt. He was covered in liver spots, wearing triple bifocals, and using a walker with tennis balls on the bottom. I kept walking, trying hard to catch someone…hell anyone else's attention.

"You heard him puta!" Mauricio forcefully grabbed my arm, pulling me toward the old man. I'd been around here long enough to learn that puta meant whore. I swallowed hard and mustered a smile.

"Come on daddy; let me take good care of you." I helped him stand, guided him out of the parlor, and into one of the rooms.

Once inside the bedroom, I closed my eyes and pretended I was still a call girl. In those days, I did what I had to in order to provide for my family. Gradually, I moved my body into an S motion. Next, I played with my nipples then bent and spread my cheeks. I couldn't tell if he was aroused or not but there was a small wet spot on his pants. I wanted to gag in disgust; I didn't know if it was ejaculation or urine. I doubted this man still had sperm. With that in mind, I resolved the wet spot was the latter of the two. "Are you ready for all of this?" I went over to the bed and lay upside down.

"No sex." He walked over and stopped at my head.

"Oh, you want a blow job?" I watched him unzip his pants prepared to tea bag me or so I thought. Nothing could prepare me for what happened next. This old bastard pulled his pants and underwear down then turned around, spread his ass cheeks, and you know what happened next. He dropped his ass right onto my lips!

INDIA

Chapter Thirty-Four
Nikki

The next day, I pulled up to the gate and waited for the security guard to permit me to enter. Anjela owned an upscale condominium in Romulus. Yesterday, she invited me over for lunch and to meet her new beau. "Here you are Ms." He slapped a visitor sticker on my window then beckoned me on. I was familiar with the complex so finding her unit took no time. Stepping from the car, I grabbed a bottle of Merlot then proceeded to the door. The wind chime hanging from her door swung in the wind as I rang the doorbell. "One minute." Anjela's voice sang from the inside. I perceived she was in a good mood. Moments later, she stood in the doorway rocking an oversized business shirt, white biker shorts, and an apron that read: kiss the cook.

"What's up Susie homemaker?" Stepping in for a hug, I was greeted with a delicious aroma. There was no way my cousin cooked this meal. She barely knew how to boil minute rice.

"Hey cuz! Come on in." Taking the bottle from me, she closed the door. "Carter is in the shower. He'll be down in a minute."

"So he lives here now?" I followed her into the

mid-sized kitchen, taking a seat at the breakfast nook, which was being used as a dinette set.

"It's just temporary." She placed the bottle into the freezer. "He's here so often to work on the case that I figured he could stay with me rather than racking up hotel bills."

"So what's for dinner?"

"Braised lamb chops, risotto, and a side salad." Like Vanna White, she flourished her hand across the food resting on the stove.

"Sounds good baby. I'm starving." Carter entered the room with a chuckle. He was wearing a Lakers t-shirt, matching basketball shorts, white socks, and Adidas house shoes. "Hello, I'm Carter; you must be Nikki."

"Yeah, I'm Nikki." While attempting to be discreet, I studied the stranger. There was something so familiar about him. I'd seen him before, I just couldn't place when or where.

"Anjela tells me so much about you." He took a seat at the table.

"I hope it's been all good." I glanced over at my cousin who was bringing the food to the table.

"Nothing too bad." He laughed. "Seriously, she did tell me you're working on a book manuscript. That's pretty interesting. If you don't mind me asking, what will the book be about?"

"My life." I could tell he was waiting for a more detailed explanation–I didn't offer one. I didn't feel comfortable sharing the intimate details of my life with a fucking federal agent. "So Carter, where are you from?" It was time to start my own line of questioning.

"I'm originally from Detroit but I was raised in California by my father." He began putting food on his plate.

"Do you have any siblings?" I didn't notice the way Anj looked at me with the side eye.

"I have a brother."

"Carter is a twin." Anjela removed the bottle from the freezer then poured everyone a glass.

"A twin? Imagine that." I picked-up my glass and took a sip.

"Yeah, my brother's name is Cartier. When our parents split up, I went with dad and he was raised by our mother." The mention of Cartier's name nearly caused me to choke. He was the man I saw Gucci hugged up with outside of the hair salon. He and his twin brother were identical.

"Where is your brother now? Are the two of you close?" Something fishy was going on around here.

"I don't know where my brother is." The way he shifted his eyes told me he was lying. "He went his own way and I went mine."

"You're not curious about what he's doing, or at least wanted to find him?"

"Quite frankly, no." I could discern I had made him uncomfortable. Anjela could tell too.

"No one said if they liked the food or not." She smiled. I wanted to tell her to call the restaurant and thank the chef who prepared it but kicked her under the table instead.

"It's really good. You'll have to share this recipe with me."

"Oh, I will." She kicked me back.

The remainder of the dinner went effortlessly. I wasn't done grilling his ass but decided to let up for now. There was something about him; I just hadn't put my finger on it. After leaving Anjela, I decided to stop by and visit with my mother-in-law. On the way over, I received a private call. "Hello."

"Hey beautiful!" Maine's voice was electrifying.

"Hey yourself!" I blushed for no reason.

"I was calling to see if you wanted to meet me for dinner."

"I just finished dinner about an hour ago." All of a sudden, I lost the compulsion to visit Claudia.

"That's cool. I like dessert better anyway." The

way he pronounced the word dessert sent chills down my body. "Meet me at The Westin Book Cadillac downtown."

"Right now?" Glancing over my attire, I noted I was underdressed. Typically, a pair of jeans, t-shirt, and gym shoes weren't date attire. However, since we were only friends, I saw no harm.

"I'll be waiting out-front." He hung up.

Sure as shit, when I pulled up to the hotel, he was standing there puffing on a cigar. The black slacks, black button-down shirt, and royal blue blazer looked good on him. I've never seen him in anything other than business attire. It was a major turn on too. "You look nice!"

"As do you." He put the cigar out and held the door open. I followed him through the lobby and pass the restaurant on the main level. I started to ask why we weren't dining there but kept my mouth closed. On the way to the room, I tried to calm my nerves. There was no telling what would happen once we were behind closed doors. "Do I make you nervous?" His finger grazed my neck, causing the hair on my head to stand up.

"Not at all." I lied, stepping from the elevator.

"Good." He laughed then slid his key into the door where we were standing.

Crossing the threshold, I was flabbergasted at

the sight before me. Several cakes, pies, and danishes were lined along the dining table. There was even a bouquet of pink carnations in the middle of all the desserts. "All of this for me?"

"I forgot to ask what types of dessert you liked so I had the restaurant send everything on the menu."

"You didn't have to go to this extreme. A cupcake would've been sufficient." I turned around with a giggle. The look in his eyes spoke volumes. He wanted me and I wanted him. When he leaned in for a kiss, I didn't resist. Somehow, we ended up engrossed in a full-blown sex scene. He ripped my blouse and pulled my jeans down. I removed his shirt and tugged at his jeans. Just when I unfastened the button he stopped. "What's wrong?" I inquired. Maine said nothing. Instead he covered his mouth with the palm of his, gazing down at my round stomach in disbelief.

"You're pregnant!?"

Chapter Thirty-Five
Gucci

"I can't believe you haven't run into your boy yet." Cartier spoke from his seat on the toilet as I entered the bathroom. He was reading the Detroit Free Press with a glock resting on his lap. I smirked to myself because my boo was too damn hood for his own good. Cartier wasn't the type of nigga to get caught slippin' so he carried a piece of steel everywhere.

"That's not my boy." I rolled my eyes then went to brush my teeth at the Jack and Jill double vanity marble sink. As far as I was concerned, if I never saw his ass again, it would be too soon. He'd been blowing my phone up to the degree that I had to change my number.

Cartier tossed his newspaper into the copper wastebasket then wiped his ass.

"I hate that fucker with a passion." I rinsed my mouth with faucet water.

"You ain't playing lil' mama, huh?" Cartier stood from the toilet seat then stepped straight into the shower; it was his ritual. Anytime he took a shit at home, he had to shower afterwards.

"Hell no! Not only am I not playing, I won't stop until I see that nigga broke." For nearly two months, Cartier and I had been growing the new empire. My mission was to put Mario's ass out of business for good. So far the plan was working.

"You look sexy as fuck when you get mad." Cartier stared at me through the clear shower glass. "You should come take a shower with me." The steam crept throughout the custom bathroom. Water dripped from his sculpted body. I was definitely turned on. As I contemplated my man's offer, I heard the doorbell.

"I'll get it." I tightened the belt on my leopard robe, prepared to answer the door, but Cartier stopped me.

"You better act like you have some sense and check that surveillance camera first."

Grabbing the remote control, I turned the television on, which was located inside the vanity mirror. There stood Claudia with her arms folded and a scowl on her face. "Shit!" I cursed; I was not in the mood for her drama today. Ever since our confrontation a few months back when I dog checked her, we've steered clear of one another. The fact that she was standing on my doorstep was out of the blue. "Baby, it's Maria's grandmother. I'll be back."

"Don't take too long." He called out as I headed down the grand spiral staircase.

As I reached the custom Italian inspired foyer, the doorbell rang again. I started to make her wait a little longer but decided against it. "Claudia, come in." I put on my best million dollar smile, batting my eyelashes for dramatic effect.

"Gucci, you look nice." She complimented while taking in the sight before her. My new house was immaculate and she was sick about it. Cartier promised to upgrade my life and give me the things I deserved once I became his girl. The mansion he purchased for me was built from the ground up and sat on a half acre lot. Cartier served it up proper with the house but he didn't stop there. Every article of clothing, every piece of furniture, and every car in the driveway was brand spanking new–customized just for me. He told me to donate my old shit to charity and that's exactly what I did.

"No offense but how do you know where I live? And how did you get pass the gate?" I didn't care how rude I may have sounded; I needed some answers.

"Well..." She started, a bit taken aback by my bluntness. "Mario gave me the address and your gate was open."

I wanted to ask her how in the hell Mario knew where I lived. Instead, I asked, "So what brings you by?" I didn't have time for small talk.

"I came over to see my granddaughter. Also, Mario wanted me to come by and see if it would be okay to pick up Maria so he could see her." She paused nervously.

"Tell Mario if he really wanted to see her, then he would've come and picked her up himself."

"Gucci, why are you being so difficult?" She frowned and I lightly chuckled. "He's been trying for a while now to see his daughter."

"Listen," I smiled. "I'm not being difficult; I'm keeping it real. Mario won't show up here because he knows I got a real nigga now! That's why his bitch ass sent you. Tell him to come ring this doorbell his self if wants to see my daughter, and then I'll think about it."

"It's not fair to Maria to keep her away from her father for your own selfish reasons!" Claudia was pissed. Silently, I wanted her to jump stupid. I would've been all over her ass in a Detroit minute.

"Call it what you want but I'm her mother and what I say goes."

"He's her father and he deserves to see her!" She yelled. Right on queue, Cartier walked down the stairs holding Maria who had awakened from her slumber. She was now eight months old and her new favorite word was daddy. It didn't matter who you were, she just liked to say daddy. She even calls me daddy sometimes but I wasn't about to let Claudia in on the secret.

Just as Cartier reached the last step, Maria uttered her favorite word as he cradled her up against his chest like she was his own. Claudia's eyes bugged from her head. "You got my grandbaby calling another man daddy?"

Chapter Thirty-Six
Mina

The hospital called last night and informed us that Samantha was ready to come home. We were elated! Her room was prepared and awaiting her arrival. "Are you ready?" I asked Sam who was running around the house like a crazy person.

"Do we have everything?" He looked at me.

"All we needed to pick up was a car seat," I laughed.

"Did we get it?"

"Of course we did!" Last week we went on a shopping spree for baby Samantha. We had bottles, blankets, clothes, a crib, a car seat, as well as a whole bunch of shit she didn't need. "Baby, let's go already!" I was anxious.

"We forgot to baby proof the house." He looked frantic. "I saw something on television about that shit."

"Sam, she's only an infant. We won't have to baby proof until she starts crawling."

"Well, it's never too soon."

"Boy stop it! I'm about to leave without you." Opening the door, I jumped at the sight of Mario.

"Hey Mina," he nodded. "Sam, I'm about two seconds from killing Gucci. I need you to be the voice of reason dog." He barged inside without an invitation. "My mama went to see Maria and she said Gucci got my daughter calling her nigga daddy! Can you believe that shit?"

"Damn homey!" Sam looked pass him toward me. His eyes begged for five minutes. My eyes indicated he only had two before I left.

"I swear I'm gonna have somebody hurt her."

"Don't speak like that big homey." Sam tried to calm him down but Mario was all the way turned up.

"I've tried to be the bigger person and let shit slide but the bitch is dirty! She stole my money but I let it go. She took my deal with a new connect; I even let that go. Nik been wanting me to leave the game anyway so I wasn't trippin'! But now she got my baby girl callin' another man daddy–that's unacceptable!

It was none of my business but Mario was right. Gucci had changed the game with this one. It wasn't cool; I felt for him. "Baby, you stay here. I'll go and pick Samantha up myself."

"Are you sure?"

"Yeah, it's fine." I knew his friend needed consoling. It was no problem to pick up the baby. Furthermore, I couldn't wait any longer.

Chapter Thirty-Seven
Nikki

"She said what?" I asked Claudia to repeat what she just told me about her visit with Gucci. However, before she had time to, my line clicked. It was Maine. Instantaneously, a smile lit up my face. "Ms. C, can I call you right back? This is my cousin." I don't even think I waited for an answer before clicking over. "Hey."

"Hey baby. What are you doing?" Maine's voice always melted my panties.

"Nothing really, except emailing my cousin the completed manuscript of my novel." The day had finally come; it was finished. Now it was up to Anjela to do her thing and see what happens.

"Congratulations sweetheart! How's my baby?" After he discovered my secret that night at the hotel, there was no alternative other than to spill the beans. It would've been wrong to lie about it, especially since he just lost a child.

"The baby is fine." I closed the laptop, lying back across the bed. Mario was gone and Junior was playing on my floor with his toys.

"When is your next appointment? I want to be there." He was excited; however, I wasn't.

"Maine, I haven't told Mario that we've been in

contact. Therefore, you just can't be showing up to appointments."

"I thought you said he knew you were carrying my seed?"

"He does know but we had plans to raise the child as ours. I didn't know you would pop back into the picture."

"Well I'm back; so you can tell dude to step back!"

"Maine," I sighed. This is where shit gets complicated.

"What Nikki? I know you don't expect me to sit back and watch another nigga raise my shorty!" As he spoke, I thought about the current situation Mario is experiencing with Gucci and Cartier. Maine was right, it wouldn't be fair. Now I was between a rock and a hard place.

"I'm not saying that. I'm just asking you to be patient with me."

"Alright I can do that, but my patience is short, so you better expedite this shit."

"Thank you for understanding." Times like this reminded me of why I fell for him in the first place.

"Nik!" Mario called out as he came through the front door. *Shit!* I hadn't even heard him pull up.

"Maine, I'll call you later!" I hung up the phone then deleted the call from my log like a scared little kid. "I'm up here. What's wrong?" I placed the phone on the nightstand just in the nick of time.

"I'm gonna fuck around and murk Gucci's ass."

"Don't talk like that." I slid onto the edge of the bed.

"Do you know what she did?"

"Yes. Your mother told me." I watched him remove his shoes.

"How dare she!?" He tossed the shoe across the room. Junior knew it was time to get out of dodge. He collected his toys then politely walked across the hallway into his room.

"Mario calm down. She can't keep Maria from you; call an attorney." I would've recommended my cousin but she was no longer a fan of Mario's. After what he did last year, she was left with a bad taste in her mouth.

"I don't want a lawyer all up in our shit like that."

"Have you tried being civil when you call her?" I knew Mario had a bad temper. Most times, it got the best of him.

"Of course I have!" He lay back on the bed. "I

wanna do some foul shit to that bitch. But then I think about you and my kids." He leaned over and kissed my stomach. "Some days, y'all are the only ones that's keeping me sane."

I wanted to tell him about Maine. How could I, particularly after a moment like this.

Chapter Thirty-Eight
Gucci

After my run-in with Claudia earlier, I'd been patiently waiting on my phone to ring. I knew Mario would be calling and going off. Amazingly, the phone hadn't rung all day. "Gucci come on." Cartier called up the stairs.

"I'm coming!" I yelled back. "Sophia, please call if Maria gets fussy." I waved goodbye to my baby. She was playing with her nanny as I headed down the stairs.

"'Bout damn time!" Cartier hit the lock on the custom 2014 white and chrome Jeep Commander.

"Why we gotta ride in this? I wanna take the Mercedes G-Wagon." I smacked my lips. Shit, I was looking fresh to death in a fitted white linen pant suit, red bra, and red Alexander McQueens. Cartier looked amazing in a pair of white Akoo jeans, white Polo top, and a crisp pair of Nike Air Force Ones. We looked liked a million bucks. It was only fitting that our whip matched our appearance.

"Gucci, you should know better!" He frowned.

"What?" I wanted everyone to see me riding around and flexing hard. I needed niggas to know I would be on top with or without Mario.

"First of all, you never take your best shit

around your workers." He started the engine.

"Why?" I asked, baffled.

"Because it only reminds them they ain't got what you got. Jealousy will make a nigga bite the hand that feeds him." He pulled a freshly rolled blunt filled with grand daddy purps from behind his ear and lit it. "Second of all, do you realize how stupid it would be to drive a Benz to the trap to pick up drug money?"

"I didn't even think about that." I replied, feeling shamefaced.

Allegedly, overnight my new organization had monopolized the streets. Every dope dealer in Michigan was buying from us. Our prices were so low, there was no competition. Mario did his best to remain in the game. Luckily, it was just a matter of time before he folded like a little bitch. It was amusing. I relished in the money, power, and respect that accompanied our connection. Conversely, everybody knows more money almost always brings more problems. Our names created jealousy amongst our enemies. Cartier thought we were untouchable. In contrast, I was constantly watching my back.

As we rode down Telegraph Road, the gaslight came on. Cartier pulled up to the BP station and jumped out. I stayed inside, playing Candy Crush on my phone. The game was flat-out addictive. *Tap. Tap.* I looked toward the window to see a bum standing there with Windex and a roll of paper towel. "I can shine these windows for five dollars." He sprayed the cleaning solution then began cleaning.

"Look nigga!" I rolled my window down. "Ain't nothin' wrong with my fuckin' windows. You need to bounce!" In Detroit everybody had a hustle, even the bums.

"Chill little mama. I'm just trynna get some lunch." He continued wiping the windshield like I hadn't just said stop. I rolled the window down further so I could reach out and shoo his ass away. Shockingly, he reached inside the roll of paper towel and produced a pistol. "Get out with your hands up bitch! You know what it is!"

"Are you fucking serious?" I was about to laugh. "You don't know who you're fucking with!"

"Bitch, I know who you are. Now give me the jewels." He kept looking back to see if anyone was coming.

"I ain't giving up shit!" I barked. "If you want 'em, you're gonna have to kill me." The look in my eyes dared him to make a move. He apprehensively dwelled on what to do.

"Not a problem. There's a price on your head

anyway." He raised the gun to my head then pulled the trigger. *Click.* It was jammed. I took the opportunity to jump out the car then commenced to whooping his ass.

"Who sent you?" I asked after taking his pistol and busting him upside the head with it.

"I ain't no snitch!" He coughed up blood. "Just know your days are numbered!"

"So are yours!" I unjammed the gun then aimed it directly at his head.

"G, no!" Cartier called from the doorway of the gas station. I looked away for a brief second, which gave the nigga on the ground a chance to get away. "What are you doing!?"

"That nigga just tried to kill me!" I screamed, pissed that I let homeboy get away.

"Get in the car. We have to toss the gun." He didn't even bother pumping the gas he had just paid for.

"What about him?" I pointed down the street.

"Fuck him; don't you hear those sirens?"

Chapter Thirty-Nine
Lovely

Today my heart was heavy with grief; my mind filled with regret. Had I just stayed my ass home and dealt with my issues, I wouldn't have been in this situation. Because of the suicide note, my family thought I was dead. Accordingly, there was probably no one searching for me. "Forty-Two." Those numbers were beginning to make me ill. I looked up to see who had spoken them and was shocked to find Santiago standing there. "Come with me."

Although confused about the request, I stood from the bed right away. He had never spoken to me or even made eye contact the entire time I was here.

"Where are we going?" I followed him to a part of the house I'd never seen, but knew it was there. We just weren't allowed to be in that area.

"Rule number one. Don't ask any questions." He responded without turning around. I'm not gonna lie I was terrified. There was something about him that was dark and daring. Perhaps, it was the way his thick brows gathered together or the coldness of his eyes. I was positively alerted to the fact that he was the bolder brother compared to

Mauricio. He always dressed in suits and never smiled. He kind of reminded me of a young Al Pacino in the movie Scarface.

As we entered what appeared to be a study then walked through unto a balcony, I shuddered apprehensively. I didn't know if it was the chill of the night or the possibility of him murdering me. "Are you cold?" His expression softened. I was too afraid to respond verbally. Therefore, I nodded. He removed his suit jacket and placed it around my shoulders. "It looks good on you." He traced the outline of the jacket with his index finger. "You're beautiful. Do you know that?"

"Thank you." I mumbled still trying to figure out where this was going.

"What's your name?" He pulled a cigar from his pocket and lit it. It was a *Gurka, His Majesty's Reserve.* I recognized the seven-hundred fifty dollar cigar because they were Maine's favorite. Each cigar was infused with Louis XIII Cognac. The strong aroma filled my nostrils, reminding me of home.

"My name is Lovely."

"Encantadora." He blew smoke out into the night. "That's how you say your name in Spanish. My name is Santiago. Mauricio is my brother." His native tongue was present but his English was still good. "He did a very bad thing by bringing you here Lovely." He took another puff then exhaled. "You see, the house of whores was a place designed for street walkers and lowly women. We take them from the gutter and bring them here." Santiago flicked the ashes, reached into his pants pocket, then handed me a piece of paper.

With my hands trembling, I unfolded it to reveal a missing flyer with my picture on it. It was a picture I'd taken on my birthday last year. Tears crept to the sides of my eyes. This confirmed my family was searching for me. They had even put up $10,000 dollars in reward money. "Lovely, I have to be honest with you." Santiago put out the cigar. "Now that you've seen our faces, know our names, as well as what goes on around here, I can't allow you to leave."

"I swear on my life, I won't say one word!" That was the truth so help me god.

"I'm sorry; I can't. However, I do have a proposal for you." He stepped into my personal space. "I will agree to remove you from the whorehouse if you agree to be my woman."

"Santiago..." I paused, shocked to hear what he had just articulated.

"I did my research on you. You're a fugitive from the United States, a drug dealer, and a cold-blooded killer! I like that," he smiled. "With a woman like you by my side, I can take over the world." Picking me up, he sat me atop the cold concrete banister. Gently, he palmed my ass while planting soft kisses over my body. "Your black skin is so damn sexy."

I didn't know what to say, but I was enjoying the moment. To my astonishment, my body responded well to his. It was the first time I'd had sex willingly in a very long time. I had no idea what I was getting myself into–right now it didn't even matter.

Chapter Forty
Mina

Ding. Dong. Someone pressed the doorbell. I was on a video chat with a potential client looking to purchase a commercial property. "Mr. Wang. I'll get that information right over to you. After you look it over, please contact me if you would like me to make an offer," I smiled.

"Okay Amina. I'll speak with you some time tomorrow." He waved goodbye then clicked off. Mr. Wang owned a large chain of convenience stores across the Midwest. He was looking to bring his business to Michigan. Hilda, my boss assigned me the project. I didn't want to let her down. Additionally, the commission would be very lucrative. Ding. Dong.

"I'm coming." I scurried to the door to see what the emergency was. To my surprise Sam's baby's mother, Tynika was standing there. "Can I help you?"

"We came to see his father." Her arms were folded like she was disappointed to see me.

"Well his father is out at the moment. What can I do for you?" I folded my arms to mimic her gesture.

"He needs to spend more time with his son."

She barged pass me and into my house. "Damn, this is how y'all living?"

"Tynika, Solomon can stay but you need to leave." I pointed toward the door.

"I can't believe this nigga got me staying in the hood and he has your ass laid up in this big ole house." She ignored my request and continued to walk through my shit.

"Look that ain't my problem. And again, you need to leave."

"Make me!" She looked at me with a raised eyebrow. I didn't have time for the games and I wasn't into catfights. Waltzing over to the phone I proceeded to dial 911. Lucky for her, Sam walked through the door.

"Tynika, what are you doing here?" He was shocked to see her.

"You haven't seen your son Sam. What's up with that?"

"What are you talking about? I just picked him up from daycare and brought him to your job the other day." He picked his son up then hugged him.

"Yeah, but you ain't been by the house to see him." She looked him over seductively. I could feel my temperature rising.

"I can't be kicking it at your crib! I'm about to get married." He pointed to me.

"What she got that I ain't got?" Tynika pouted. "I had your firstborn son. What did she do?"

"Bitch, you got three seconds to bounce!" I was about to snap.

"Tynika, don't come around here with all that shit! When it comes to Solomon, I do what I'm supposed to. But I don't want you!" Sam walked over to the door, holding it open.

"Sam don't fuck with me or I will turn you in!"

"I've paid you way more than what you would've gotten in child support court. So go ahead and turn me in," he dared her.

"Without receipts, you can't prove you paid me a fuckin' dime," she cackled.

"Bitch you need to leave!" I lunged across the room but Sam prevented my fist from connecting with her face. I didn't take kindly to threats about my man.

"If you lay one finger on me, I'll send your ass to jail too!"

INDIA

Chapter Forty-One
Nikki

Finally my novel, *Memoirs of a Hood Wife: The Autobiography of Nikki Wallace*© had been picked up by a major publishing house. Within days of Anjela shopping it, I had a deal. It hit bookstores nationwide almost immediately. Response from the readers was unreal. One single day after releasing the book, I was on the New York Times Best Seller list. Critics couldn't comprehend why an urban novel was receiving so much attention. What they failed to realize was my *Memoirs* were real, raw, and relatable. In every hood or underprivileged community across America was a hood wife handling the inner workings of her husband's hustle. It didn't matter if she was the person standing at the stove cooking crack or riding dirty down the highway transporting contraband. A hood wife knows her position and plays it well. Nevertheless, living the glamorous life comes with incredible sacrifices. It took a bullet and practically losing my life to realize being a hood wife didn't exemplify all I thought it would.

"What you doing cuz?" Anjela stepped into my bedroom. I was packing for a weekend trip to promote the book in New York as well as reading emails on my phone.

"I'm just packing. What's up?" Not awaiting a response, I continued to read emails.

"I wish I was going with you. Is Mario going?"

"No, he's going to stay behind and watch Junior. Claudia went on a bingo trip. She'll be gone the whole weekend."

"What are you wearing to the signing?" She asked. I didn't respond because I was too engrossed with my email message.

"What are you reading? It must be important because you're certainly ignoring me." She grabbed my phone, reading the message aloud. *"Dear Nikki, My name is Dee-Dee; I'm twenty-two years old. I'm from Flint, Michigan but currently locked up at a Virginia State Correctional Facility for women. I was arrested on my nineteenth birthday for assisting my fiancé with disposing of a body. I didn't kill anyone. All I did was drive the car, and for that I'm serving life behind bars."* Anjela looked at me with widened eyes. *"Initially, we fled our hometown on some real Bonnie and Clyde type shit. But it didn't take long for the police to find us. My fiancé told me he couldn't do jail and committed suicide on the morning we had agreed to turn ourselves in. Imagine that! Here I was being a ride or die bitch on the run from the law and thinking the shit was cute. Then this mofo takes the easy way out. Leaving me alone, scared, and helpless."* Anjela paused again, this time her mouth was wide open. *"Anyway, for three years I sat here angry at him and everybody else. Then I read your book and it made me think. I'm in this predicament because of me! No one forced me to drive the car. No one forced me to flee the state. Those were all decisions I made as a "Hood Wife." Girl, if I could've gotten ahold of your book three years ago, my life would undeniably be different. I would've realized ain't no title worth spending the rest of my life in jail for."* Angela stopped reading then handed the phone back. Her eyes were moist, so were mine. "Damn cuz, that shit was deep!" She sniffed.

"You're telling me!" I had to take a seat on the bed to collect my thoughts.

"All jokes aside, when you said you wanted to write a book, I didn't believed you would actually impact people with your story," she disclosed.

"On a regular basis, I get tons of messages like this."

"Damn, who knew there were so many hood wives around the world?" She stated.

"There's a secret society of us." Placing the phone down to continue packing, it rang. It was Maine. "Hello."

"Hey, are you all packed for New York?" He was excited about the invitation I'd extended to him a few days ago.

"Just about." I used as few words as possible. Anjela was all up in my grill.

"Good! I'll see you at the airport in the morning." He reported then ended the call.

"Who was that?" She reached for the phone but I was too fast.

"None of your business."

"Mario is going to whip your ass." She shook her head with a giggle.

"Why is Mario gon' do that?" He walked into the room.

"I was showing her my dress for the event tomorrow. Anj said you wouldn't approve." Thinking fast, I removed a black and silver sheer dress with rhinestones from the closet. It wasn't at all what I planned to wear. At the moment, it was the only skimpy dress I could find.

"Hell no, you ain't wearing that without me." He removed the dress from my hand then placed it back into the closet. "I'll help you find something else."

"Ok cuz. Have a safe flight and call me once you land." She collected her items and left the room.

"Here is something more appropriate." Mario stepped out of the closet with a red cocktail dress.

"Thanks baby but I had a second option already." I zipped up the luggage and sat it on the floor.

"Me and Junior should fly out there for your big event." Mario sat on the bed.

"Huh?" I damn near choked.

"I was thinking about it; I would hate for you to be out there all alone."

"I'm a big girl; I'll be fine." Leaning over, I kissed his lips. "Anyway, it's only for a day."

"I guess you're right." He rubbed my ass.

"So what will you and Junior get into in my absence?" I sat on top of his lap, straddling him.

"I don't know." He shrugged, lifting me off his lap.

"Where are you going?"

"I have to holla at Gucci." He went into the closet safe and retrieved two guns.

"Mario please don't do anything stupid."

INDIA

Chapter Forty-Two
Gucci

I was shaken after the run-in at the gas station but the day had to go on. Cartier thought it was only a bluff from some young niggas trying to flex. I knew better though. Over the years, I'd managed to piss off a lot of people. Therefore, I doubted it was an idle threat. It could've been anybody with a grudge. I intended to discover who it was before they could try me again. "I shouldn't be long." Cartier got out of the car and ran into the house. It was our last stop for the day, and I was ready to get back home. After about twenty minutes, I stepped from the car to see what the hold-up was. That's when I spotted Mario coming up the block; I knew this meant trouble.

The black Hummer was speeding. I didn't have to see his expression behind the tinted windows. I was aware he was beyond pissed. SCREECH! His tires came to a smoking stop then he jumped out like a madman. I was standing on the porch with nowhere to run. "What's up with all that shit you was talking?"

"Mario you better get away from me with all that shit. Cartier is right inside the house."

"Tell that nigga to come outside; he can get it

too!" He beat on his chest like a gorilla. "I'm done fucking with you bitch! You ain't shit but a dirty, grimey, slime ass hoe!"

"Words don't hurt me nigga!" I lied. Truthfully, his words stung deeply. I felt like I was being rebuked by my father.

"What the fuck is going on out here?" Cartier stepped onto the porch with a gun.

"So we pullin' pistols now?" Mario reached into his waistband, retrieving two. "I got one for you and one for that bitch!"

"You talking real reckless for a nigga on my block," Cartier laughed. Mario was outnumbered.

"This might be your block but I came with my own killas." He pointed toward the street where four carloads of men sat idling.

"Are we gon' hold court in the street or sit down like men?" Cartier asked.

"Dog, I been as much of a man as I'm gon' be. I've been calling Gucci trying to see my daughter. She on some power trip and I'm fed up."

"Put the guns away and let's talk about it." Cartier slid his gun back into the holster.

"My man, we ain't got shit to talk about except when the fuck I'ma see my daughter." Mario didn't drop either of his weapons.

"That can be arranged!" Cartier looked at me.

"Swing by the crib tomorrow. I'll have her ready for you." I smacked my lips.

"I want to see my daughter NOW!" He folded his arms.

"Obviously, you know where we live. Head on over. I'll call the nanny and tell her to let you in," Cartier avowed.

"What!" Smacking my lips and with my hands on my hips, I shot a disapproving glance his way.

"Cool." Mario turned then headed back to his vehicle.

"I'm going too!" I headed off the porch.

"Why?" Both Mario and Cartier said in unison.

"I'm not gon' give you the opportunity to kidnap my child."

"You ain't ridin' with me!" Mario shook his head.

"To hell I'm not." Once he unlocked the car, I opened the passenger door and hopped in. "Cartier, I'll grab one of the other cars and be back in an hour."

We were twelve minutes into the ride before Mario broke the silence. "What happened to you?"

"The world!" I retorted.

"That's a shame G. You was good people. Now you a straight up bitch!"

"Mario don't start name-calling because I have

few names for you."

"Go ahead; get that shit off your chest. Maybe it'll make you feel better." He turned the music down.

"After everything you put me through, you should be the one talking." I was beyond bothered and trying to keep from socking this man.

"Gucci, I've said I'm sorry dozens of times. If it'll make you feel better, I'll say it once more." He sighed then glanced at me. "I'm sorry. I never should've led you to believe our relationship could work. We never should've crossed that line. I can see how bad I hurt you; and I wish you knew it was never my intention to do so. I love you girl." He tried to pat my shoulder but I moved away.

"You don't love me so stop lying!" I could feel the tears welling up behind my eye sockets.

"I do love you!" He paused. "I may not love you the same way I love Nikki but I do love you. You were my ace, my best friend, and my partner. Me and you were like this." He crossed his index and middle finger. "It kills me that we're on different sides now. But I understand and acknowledge it was entirely my fault. I have to take ownership of my shit. That's why I let you slide with taking the money. It's also why I let you live after stealing the deal with Bayani." He turned to face me again. "The only thing I couldn't let you slide with is keeping my daughter away from me. That shit ain't cool!"

"Mario, I knew that was the only way to hurt you. I wasn't gon' keep her from you forever. But I did want you to feel my wrath."

"And you got her calling another man daddy!" He shook his head. I wanted to let him in on the secret; instead, I changed the subject.

"How is the organization?" It was a sour subject but I needed to get the attention off of me.

"Those who chose to remain loyal are good. Them others nigga's jumped ship."

"I'm surprised you haven't walked away yet." The tension in the car had diminished slightly.

"I ain't no quitter. I started from the bottom once before so it's nothing. I got some shit lined up. Once I put my team back on, then I'll leave." He exited the freeway.

"How does Nikki feel about it?"

"We really shouldn't be talking about her." There was a pause before he asked, "How's homeboy treating you?"

"We shouldn't be talking about him either," I giggled. "He treats me good though."

"That's good!" Mario smirked. It was difficult to tell if he was genuinely happy though.

"He's everything I always wanted; so I can't complain."

"I'm glad to hear you're happy G. All I ask is that you watch your back with him." Mario cut on the blinker and headed down the street leading to my house.

"What's that supposed to mean?"

"I'm just saying something seems shady with him that's all." Mario pulled up to the gate which was open. I could've sworn I scolded the guard earlier when Claudia came over about this same thing. "He shows up out of the woodwork, finds you, and starts splurgin' on you like crazy within a meager two months. Did he tell you where his money came from?"

"He has some business dealings in Cali."

"So why did he need your connect if he had his own?" Mario stepped from the vehicle. "If he was doing it on a grand scale in California, why on earth would he ever come back to Detroit? If anything, he would've moved you to his spot." Mario's words didn't sit well with me.

"Whatever! You're just a hater." I unlocked the door.

"Never that!" He shook his head. "I'm just keeping it one hundred."

Chapter Forty-Three
Mina

Three days had passed since Tynika dropped Solomon off. She didn't leave him with a diaper bag so we had to run out to the store. We purchased clothes, diapers, and milk. For the most part, he was okay but today he woke up screaming and wouldn't stop. "Have you tried calling her again?" I asked Sam while rocking him back and forth.

"Yeah, I've called so much now her fucking phone is going to voicemail." He retrieved the baby from my arms and tried rocking him to give me a break.

"I have a showing today but I'm going to call one of the other agents to see if she can go on my behalf."

"No, go ahead and go to work. I got this."

"There is no way you can handle two babies Sam." Shaking my head, I grabbed the phone and proceeded to call the office.

When I came back into the room, Solomon had turned it up a notch. Sam was frustrated so I took him into my arms then carried him into Samantha's room. I rummaged through her dresser and retrieved a thermometer. Solomon didn't feel warm but I had to rule everything out. I took a seat in the rocking chair, placing the stick under his tongue. After a few seconds, the digital reader said 97.1. He didn't have a fever; yet something was undeniably wrong. I went back into the bedroom and retrieved my cell phone. I googled Solomon's symptoms of a slobbery mouth, not wanting to eat, and consistent crying. The search engine provided websites for teething and constipation. One of the sites recommended Orajel and a frozen teething ring. At present, I didn't have either. In view of that, I hurried into the kitchen to fill a sandwich bag with crushed ice. Once I placed it into his mouth, miraculously the crying stopped. *Thank God!* I took him back upstairs to lay down with his father. "I'll be back, I'm going to get what he needs for his mouth." I whispered to Sam who was already dozing off.

On my way to the store, I received a call from Gucci. "What's up girl. You sound shitty."

"I've been up all morning with a screaming baby," I yawned.

"Samantha?" She asked.

"No bitch, it's Solomon; Sam's son."

"Sam's what?"

"You heard me right."

"When did this shit happen?" She sounded as

shocked as I was.

"It's a long story. I'm headed to the store now for some teething stuff. I'll call you later."

"Ok, but I was calling to see if you wanted to go to the movies with me and Satin tonight."

"No thanks. I'm too damn tired to do anything today. Thanks for the invite though."

"Mina, come on we haven't went out in forever," she begged.

"Girl, I have two kids right now. I'm beat! All of us don't have the privilege of hiring a nanny."

"Well can we at least do breakfast tomorrow? I have a lot to tell you."

"Okay, I'll see you tomorrow. Where do you wanna go?" I pulled into the parking spot and turned the car off.

"Just come to my house. I'll have the chef cook for us while I take you on a tour." She gave me the address and we ended the call.

Chapter Forty-Four
Nikki

The London NYC was a swank hotel smack dab in the middle of New York City. With marble flooring and golden chandeliers, it represented everything elegant. I've stayed at some upscale places in my lifetime but this took the cake. The publishing house reserved a standard room for my visit. However, at check-in, Maine decided to upgrade us to the penthouse suite.

The place was absolutely stunning! It measured over 2,500 square feet spread throughout two floors of living space. Both levels were decorated with the most posh furnishings. Even the bathroom was amazing! However, my favorite part of the suite was the180 degree views of the city from bay windows. I was able to view Central Park, the Hudson River, the George Washington Bridge, as well as the Manhattan skyline.

"It's breathtaking!"

"I thought you would like it." Maine walked up behind me, wrapping his arms around my waist. Casually, I slid from his clutches and went to peer out of one of the windows. "Do I make you nervous?"

"Not really," I lied. Frankly, just the thought of

being here with him made me nervous as hell. Although we hadn't done anything since the other night, I felt like I was cheating. I liked Maine but I loved Mario. I felt I at least owed Mario a conversation before kicking things up a notch with Maine.

"So why are you running from me?" He was standing beside me at the window now.

"I'm not running from you. I'm just excited to be here that's all."

"I'm excited to be here with you, which is why I upgraded our accommodations. I wanted your visit to the Big Apple to be memorable." Slowly, his hand caressed my back.

"Thank you." Relaxing a bit, I permitted my body to give in to his touch.

Bzzzzz.

The cell phone in my pocket broke our embrace. "It's Mario." I placed an index finger to my lip to indicate silence. "Hey Rio!" I moved away from Maine, who was still making circles on my back with his finger. "Yeah, I just got here. The place is nice too. How is my baby?" I didn't miss the look Maine gave me when he thought I was referencing Mario. "Yeah, put him on for me. Hey Junior, I miss you! You're going to have so much fun with daddy!" I watched Maine walk away, disappearing into the bedroom. "Oh, your sister is there? That's nice! I love you! I'll see you tomorrow okay!" Ending the call, I returned the phone to my pocket. Mario and Gucci must've come to an agreement since Maria was spending the night. Normally, I would've called Claudia for the scoop. However, the sound of bath water caught my attention.

I walked into the bedroom and gasped. Maine was standing there in his birthday suit. "Boy, what are you doing?" I giggled.

"I saw this large jaquzzi tub and decided to take a bath. Would you care to join me?"

"Maine, we shouldn't." Guilt was really starting to set in. I believed I was betraying Mario. He was at home with the kids while I was hundreds of miles away in a penthouse with a butt naked nigga.

"Look Nikki," he sighed. "I understand you got a man at home but being here with me has to mean something." Maine stepped up into my face then bit down on his bottom lip. He slowly unbuttoned my blouse, then released each breast from the cups of my bra. Deliberately, he licked and sucked until they were erect. Next, he removed my belt and unzipped my jeans. Getting on his knees, he pulled my pants to the floor then began massaging my vagina. A wet spot quickly formed on the pink lace panties. From that point, there was no turning back. That day, we made love until the sun set and then rose in the morning.

The next day it was game time. The PR team had done an excellent job of promoting my event. I halfway expected no one to show up. Fortunately, the line formed from the door then spilled down into the next block. The readers in New York showed me lots of love. I signed books as well as snapped a few pictures. One of the local radio stations, Power 105.1 had even come down to host a live interview. The entire time Maine stayed back and out of the way. He let me do my thing. The independence felt amazing. For the first time in a long time, I was doing something that actually made me proud. No longer was I a mere hood wife, I was an entrepreneur. I wanted to demonstrate to girls in the ghetto that you didn't need a man to rise above you circumstances. You didn't need to rob for Red Bottoms. All you had to do was apply your mind.

Chapter Forty-Five
Lovely

As I lay in the arms of Santiago, who was snoring loudly and breathing heavily, my thoughts drifted to Maine. I reflected on where he was and how life had been treating him. I wondered if he was thinking of me, or if he even knew I was missing. If life had a rewind button, I would certainly go back and change things. I hated the way I allowed him to leave as well as regretted the things I said. It was too late to make things right. Nevertheless, I truly wished I somehow could just apologize. He needed to know how remorseful I was about the way we ended. Even if he had moved on, I wanted him to understand his love and kindness weren't in vain. He was a good man; and I would forever hold him in my heart.

"Encantadora what's wrong? Why aren't you sleeping?" Santiago yawned.

"Just thinking," I smiled.

"About what?" He sat up, rubbing a hand over his face to wipe sleep from his eyes. Santiago's façade was rough and ruthless. But within, he was a gentle soul. He was my knight in shining armor who rescued me and saved the day. After the night he told me he wanted me for himself, I was removed from the whore roster. He moved me up to his wing of the house and treated me exceptionally well. Mauricio was jealous of our new relationship. Lucy was flat out panicky. Now that I had free reign of the house, you should've seen her tiptoeing around me.

"Baby, it's my birthday. I want to do something other than be cooped up in here," I whined. Today was not really my birthday but I was tired of being in the house. Although I was no longer a whore, I remained a prisoner. The only scenery I'd seen since I got here was inside the house and the property outside, which was visible from the back porch. I was no longer permitted to associate with Daphnie; I was bored.

"Felize cumpleaños." He leaned over, kissing my neck. I could tell by the way he spoke them, the words translated to happy birthday. "What do you want to do today?"

"I want to go out with you and have some fun. Maybe we can walk on the beach or something." I alluded; elated he at least was considering my proposal.

"Do you promise not to do any funny business?" He sat on the side of the bed. He was naked, so was I.

"Santiago, I won't lie. I can't stand being here.

On the other hand, I do like being with you." I crawled over to his side of the bed and began kissing his back. I wasn't pretending to like him either. The man was sexy. His body was impeccable. Whenever he spoke Spanish, it sent chills over my body. He was different, yet similar to Maine. I felt a connection with him.

"Baby, that feels so good but I've got an important meeting." He stood from the bed. I watched his tight ass strut across the hardwood floor. His penis swayed like a pendulum from side to side.

"Does that mean I can't get any birthday sex?" I pretended to pout.

"I will give you plenty of that tonight after we come back from our walk on the beach," he smiled.

"Oh Santiago, thank you so much!" I jumped up on the bed and did a happy dance. Finally, I would be able to leave this house, if only for a little while.

INDIA

Chapter Forty-Six
Gucci

"Girl where are you?" Satin spoke into my receiver. She and I had a movie date tonight. "I told your ass to be here at eight."

"I'm on the way. I just have to pick up the night deposit from the club." I slid my key into the backdoor deadbolt.

"You better hurry the fuck up!" She smacked her lips. "I've been waiting to see this movie all week."

"I'm sorry but duty calls." I closed the door behind me. So busy listening to her, it didn't even dawn on me that the alarm hadn't gone off. The club was closed on Monday. Therefore, the alarm should've been set after Raven, the manager, left yesterday evening.

"Whatever just..." I never heard what she said because a jolt to my face sent the phone flying across the floor. The blow left me dazed and confused. I stumbled back a few steps, attempting to snap back. WHAM! The uppercut sent my body flying across the room just like my phone.

"You think you all that, huh? What about now!" He stumped my rib cage. I heard a crack then lost my breath shortly thereafter. The assailant punished my body with numerous punches and kicks. I was weak and defenseless.

"What do you want?"

"I want you to pay for what you did!" He kicked me again.

"Please tell me what I did and I swear I'll make it right!"

"It's too late now! You humiliated me; now it's time to humiliate you." He unzipped his pants.

"Please don't rape me," I cried.

"Don't nobody want that funk box." He removed his penis from his pants then pissed all over me. All I could do was lay there and endure it. Thankfully, the ordeal only lasted a couple of minutes but it felt much longer. Soon afterwards, the masked intruder escaped through the backdoor, leaving me curled into the fetal position. I'd been beaten to within an inch of my life. My cell phone was too far away for me to reach it; yelling for help was pointless. I just laid there and prayed someone would find me before it was too late.

Help came in the morning by way of Cartier and Mina. "Oh my god! She's in here." Mina dropped to the floor, checking me for a pulse.

"Gucci baby, wake up." Cartier slapped my face. I wanted to tell his ass to stop but the words wouldn't come. My throat was dry. "Gucci get up."

He shook me until my eyes opened.

"Who did this to you?" Mina asked with tears in her eyes.

"Mario. Please get Mario," I cried. At that moment, he was the only person I wanted to see. He would protect me.

"I'ma kill that nigga!" Cartier roared as he lifted me up. I wanted to tell him I didn't mean Mario attacked me. But then I would have to explain why I was calling for him.

"I'm going to call Pete and get you home."

"Fuck that, she needs a hospital." Cartier shook his head.

"If it's one thing I know about Gucci, she hates hospitals." Mina declared. "I'm going to call Pete; he'll handle it." Peter Jamison was one of my best clients at the Doll House. As luck would have it, he was also a physician. His specialty was Sports Medicine. Thus, bruised and broken body parts were in his wheelhouse.

All the way home, tears dangled off the edges of my lashes but I refused to allow them to fall. The pain was unbearable. I could barely breathe; and the ride was incredibly uncomfortable. My body ached like never before. I realized bones had been broken. "Gucci, I swear I'm gonna bust a cap in your boy!" Cartier shouted furiously.

"I don't think it was Mario." Mina spoke from the backseat.

"Why not? He's been talking big shit about her out in the streets. It's the only thing that makes sense," Cartier rationalized.

"Why would he do that to her after she gave him what he wanted, which was Maria?" She held an ice bag to my face. "Mario would never actually hurt Gucci."

"Mina, for his sake, you better hope you're right! But if the streets don't start talking by tonight, I'ma handle ol' boy."

Chapter Forty-Seven
Mina

I couldn't believe all the shit that had gone down yesterday. Gucci was in pretty bad shape. Pete had stitched her up and gave her some pain killers that had her drowsy. I stayed with her last night. Cartier was in no position to care for her. He was too busy trying to plot on Mario. I'd gone downstairs to warm her up some soup the chef had prepared and heard him and two goons conversing. They planned to ride by Mario's house and do a drive-by. Although it had nothing to do with me, the shit just didn't sit right in my spirit.

On my way home the next day, I deliberated if I should warn him or not. Really, it was none of my business but if there was a war being waged against him he had the right to know. "Baby how is Gucci?" Sam met me at the door.

"She's good. The doctor stitched her up and gave her something for the pain and to help her sleep."

"What happened?" He helped me take my jacket off.

"Somebody jumped her at the Doll House last night. She's pretty banged up."

"Does she know who did it?" He was a little

too concerned if you asked me.

"Her jaw is broken so she really can't talk. However, Cartier seems to think it was Mario."

"He wouldn't do no shit like that," Sam frowned.

"I know. I don't believe it either. But he does look guilty. Especially after all that reckless shit he's been talking."

"He was mad." Sam defended his friend.

"I know that but Cartier was talking about shooting up his house tonight."

"Aww, hell naw!" Sam retrieved the phone from his pocket and proceeded to dial. I really didn't want to be caught up in Gucci and Mario's drama. I decided to let Sam relay the message and went upstairs to check on the children.

As I opened the door, a smile crept over my face. Solomon was sleeping peacefully on the blow-up mattress beside his sister's crib. As of yet, we hadn't purchased a toddler bed for him. However, I planned to get one ASAP. His mother's trifling ass had pulled a disappearing act, but it was all good. I couldn't fathom loving two children whom I hadn't birthed the way I do. I guess in a crazy way I viewed them as mine. They'd both been left behind for me to raise.

Tiptoeing over to the white crib with unicorns

spinning on the mobile, I leaned over and kissed Samantha. She was knocked out but smiling. My grandmother used to tell me that's what happened when Angels talked to babies. Next, I bent down to kiss Solomon's forehead. He was a cute kid. When I stood back up, Sam was entering the room. "Shit is about to hit the fan! It may be best for you and the kids to get a hotel room for a few days."

INDIA

Chapter Forty-Eight

Nikki

On the flight back, I could tell something was up with Maine. "Are you okay?"

"Yeah, I'm good," he stated as he looked out the window.

"It doesn't seem like it."

"I'm cool, just thinking that's all."

"Thinking about what?" I didn't think he was going to make me beg for it.

"One of the last times I was on a plane Lovely was giving birth to my son." He finally looked at me. No tears fell but the corners of his eyes were moist.

"Have you called to check on her?" He informed me she was a wanted fugitive in the United States so he took her somewhere she'd be free. Maine didn't give up her exact location but my guess was Mexico. It was the obvious choice. All fugitives attempt to make it across the border.

"No. I'm done with her." He shook his head. "I left her with family so I know she's safe. There's no reason to call or go back."

"But you still love her though. I thought love was worth fighting for." I should've been applying this lecture to my own situation. My frustration with Mario in the streets was intense but I did love him. Maybe I should put my own feelings on the back burner and stick it out.

"I do love her Nikki but I'm not in love with her anymore. It's time to move on and start fresh." Maine placed his hand over my stomach. He must've sensed my apprehension. "Look ma, I ain't trynna marry you or no shit like that. I just like being in your company. You cool people and you sexy as fuck. Not to mention the fact that you're carrying my seed. If you and I are meant to be, it'll happen. If we're not, then it won't."

I didn't know what else to say so I chose to say nothing at all. As a substitute, I put on my Beats by Dre headphones, escaping into the music for the duration of the flight. At the gate, Maine and I parted ways. I promised to text when I got home, he did the same. After retrieving my suitcase, I headed toward the front door where a gentleman with dreadlocks stood holding a sign with my name on it. I was puzzled because I thought Mario was picking me up himself. After handing the man my luggage, I retrieved my phone to call home. "Damn!" The phone was as dead as a doorknob. I slid onto the backseat and gave the driver my address.

All the way home, I dreaded the conversation

Mario and I needed to have. I was nervous; my stomach was in knots. I didn't think he would handle what I had to say very well. "Ms., I can't go down your street. Should I drop you at the corner, or take you somewhere else?" The driver's voice invaded my thoughts.

"Huh?" I didn't comprehend what he was saying. "What do you mean you can't go down the street?"

"The police are everywhere; they have the street blocked off." At the mention of the police, I opened the car door in full fledged panic mode. Sure as shit, there were three squad cars and one ambulance blocking the street. To make matters worse, they were right in front of my house.

Not caring one bit about my luggage or purse being inside of the Metro Car, I took off down the street.

"What happened?" I asked a neighbor standing on the lawn with two dogs on a leash.

"All I know is I heard rapid gunfire," she shrugged.

"Oh my god!" I sped up as best I could with my limp.

"Ma'am you can't cross the tape." An officer held me back.

"My son is in there!" I screamed.

"Let her through." Another cop spoke from the side of my house. As I ran up the porch steps, he stopped me. "Ma'am that's the wrong house."

"Huh?" I stepped back and looked at the house. It was absolutely my house. What on earth was he talking about? Just as I was about to ask him, I noticed most of the commotion was actually coming from my neighbors' house. She was an older woman in her seventies who lived with her husband. Immediately, I was relieved to know the incident hadn't taken place at my home. Nevertheless, I was still concerned. I exited the porch then headed next door. The police officer had already given me permission to enter so no one tried to stop me. "Mrs. Crooks." I called out for my neighbor. She was a nice lady who I had become very fond of. She was sort of the cool-ass grandmother of the neighborhood.

"I'm in here." She called from the kitchen. When I bent the corner, there was one police officer blocking her back bedroom entrance and two emergency medical technicians attending her. She was sitting on a chair in the kitchen. The burgundy wig was crooked atop her head, and her nightgown was lifted above her waist. A bottle of Hennessey rested in her clutches, and she was smoking a joint. Mrs. Crooks was an old school gangster for real.

You have to have nerve to smoke weed in front of the cops; medical marijuana card or not. She reminded me a lot of the character Madea; always saying and doing whatever she wanted because she knew no one had the balls to stop her.

"What happened? Are you okay?" Blood was trickling down her leg.

"I'm fine Nikki. These niggas done fucked around and shot me in my ass that's all!" She took a long, hard pull on her joint then blew out several small smoke rings.

"You got shot!?" It was hard to believe.

"Yeah girl!" She flicked the funny cigarette into the ashtray. "I was lying in bed watching the news. When it went off, I rolled over to go to sleep. A few minutes later, I heard gunshots and felt a burning sensation. That's when I knew I'd caught a hot one in the ass!"

"Oh wow!" My mouth was wide-open. "Do you need me to call anyone for you?"

"No sweetie I'm good. They're gonna stitch me up then I'm going back to bed. I got church in the morning."

"Actually, Mrs. Crooks we need to get you to the hospital." One of the EMT's informed her.

"Ain't nobody got time to be going to the hospital." She shook her head.

"The bullet is still lodged in your flesh. They will have to take x-rays to see where it is and remove it."

"Child please!" She smacked her lips. "It don't even hurt. Just pour some alcohol on it and hand me a band-aid.

"Mrs. Crooks I can't do that." The EMT explained. "Can you please lie down on this stretcher for me? I need to cut your gown."

"The devil is a lie! You ain't cutting nothing I done paid good money for." She shook her head adamantly. I wanted to laugh but held it in. After a few more minutes of debating, Mrs. Crooks eventually surrendered and went to the hospital with her husband. I promised to check on her later then headed home.

Once inside the house, I could tell no one was home. I went upstairs and plugged up my cell phone. The minute it powered up, it started blowing up.

Chapter Forty-Nine
Gucci

"I'ma be fresh as hell if the feds watchin'..." The sound of my phone jolted me from a nap. A glance at the screen indicated the caller was Mario. Maybe he'd heard the news and was calling to check on me, or maybe he was calling to declare his innocence. Either way, I couldn't have answered even if I wanted to. My face was swollen and hurt like hell. In view of that, I waited for the call to end then sent him a text message: "Can't talk. What's up?" About half of a second went by before the phone beeped.

"Tell that nigga he's a dead man!" I re-read the words twice before replying.

"What are you talking about?"

"Don't act like you don't know he tried to shoot up my fucking house." By now, my heart was racing. I got ready to respond but another message came through. "It was you who said I did it. Just for that, I should handle you too!"

"Mario, I had nothing to do with this. I swear!" I slammed the phone down on the nightstand, grabbed a robe, and went to find Cartier.

As I wondered around the palatial estate, my mind raced at a million thoughts per minute. The shit was so disturbing I was beginning to get a headache. "Ms. Gucci." The housekeeper called from down the hall. "Mr. Cartier is in the sunroom asking for you."

"Okay, thank you." I mumbled with a smile, continued walking, then stopped. "Which way is the sunroom again?"

It took her a minute to understand what I was asking before she replied. "Keep going down to the end of the hall. It's the first door on the left." She smiled, then returned to complete the task she was performing.

On my way down the spacious hallway, I glanced through the glass at the gardener who was busy spreading mulch. The yard was really coming together. There were Dogwood Trees, perennials, Roses, and lots of greenery. It was absolutely beautiful. I couldn't wait for Maria to start walking so I could take her out there. *Knock. Knock.* I noticed Cartier sitting on one of the chairs with the phone up to his ear. "Good morning baby."

"What did you do!?" I was furious.

"I handled that shit! That's what I did!." I wanted to tell this nigga what he actually did was make a big fucking mess.

Chapter Fifty
Lovely

About an hour after Santiago left for his meeting, there was a knock on the bedroom door. "Come in." I didn't care who it was, I was just happy to have some company. I was in the bathroom brushing my teeth.

"Lovely, it's me." As Lucy entered, I frowned.

"What can I do for you?" I peeped my head from the bathroom door with toothbrush in hand. She was standing there dressed in lingerie as usual; I guess it was her signature look or something.

"Santiago sent me to the store for you." She sat two garment bags on the bed along with two shoe boxes.

"I didn't ask for anything from the store." I bent my head toward the sink and rinsed my mouth out. Mexican tap water tasted salty.

"He told me it was your birthday and to buy you something special." I couldn't tell if her smile was sincere or not but I let her continue. "Seeing as you two have a date night planned, I thought I'd get you something to wear." She unzipped the first garment bag to reveal a grey strapless Gucci sundress. The second garment bag held the same dress except it was white.

"Lucy this is very pretty." I favored the white one.

"I didn't know what your taste was. Therefore, I took a shot in the dark." She explained. "I also bought two different pairs of shoes. You look like you wear a size eight. If they don't fit, I'll take them back."

I opened up the first box and saw a beautiful black peep toe wedge. The second box was a simple gold sandal with rhinestones. Although the peep toes were my favorite, I chose the sandals since we were headed to the beach. "Thank you Lucy. You did a very good job." I smiled, indicating my appreciation.

"I'm glad you like them." She waved goodbye then closed the door behind her.

It took me two hours to get ready. I hadn't been on a date in so long that I was nervous. *Was my hair supposed to be up, or should I let it hang down? Should I put on make-up or just go natural?* Finally, I decided to put my hair in a simple bun and apply just a touch of lip gloss. I didn't want to wear the makeup they made us wear when entertaining. It would only serve to remind Santiago of my raunchy past.

At last, Santiago was back and it was time to go. Hand in hand, we headed out the front door and into a waiting Town Car. Mauricio was shaking his head and yelling at his older brother in Spanish. I recognized by the expression on his face he didn't think our date was a good idea. Santiago paid his brother no mind. "This means so much to me." I leaned over, planting a kiss on his lips.

"Thank me later," he winked.

The driver took the scenic route toward the beach. Gazing out of the window, I marveled at the beautiful sights before me. Mexico was an amazingly beautiful place. It felt as though I was seeing it for the first time. Within twenty minutes, we were approaching familiar territory. Up ahead, I could view the bar I was at when Mauricio drugged me. Further down was the housing development where Maine's property was located. I tried to keep from getting too excited. I didn't want Santiago to be alarmed. "There's the beach baby." He pointed as the driver parked.

"Wow! It's beautiful." I pretended it was new to me.

"Come on, I'll race you to the water." He removed his loafers and got out of the car. I removed my sandals, attempting to catch up with him but he was too fast.

"You cheated!" I was out of breath. The warm water crept up to our feet, covered our ankles, and then traveled backward.

"Come on. Let's get this walk out of the way before dinner." He grasped my hand as we headed down the beach. We walked for what appeared to be a mile before stopping at a table, two chairs, and a man in a chef's hat. At first, I was confused but then I understood. Santiago had made reservations for us to have a private dinner on the beach.

"Santiago, this is incredible!" I couldn't stop blushing.

"You deserve it." He pulled my chair out, I took a seat.

Just before the chef could place any food on my plate, something in the distance caught my eye. It was Do It and Shawnie. They were collecting seashells along the beach. The closer they got, the more afraid I became. I didn't know how this was gonna play out.

Chapter Fifty-One
Mina

Just like I knew it would, a war had been initiated between the two sides. Mario's crew had already retaliated by shooting up a few of Cartier's known hangouts. Luckily, he hadn't been hit. Nonetheless, it was just a matter of time. Had it not been for Maria, Mario would've definitely taken beef to Gucci's front door. He was a killer but he wasn't crazy. He would never put the life of his daughter in jeopardy. Sam was in and out of the hotel every night. I prayed for his safety but understood he had to do what he had to do.

In order to be with the kids, I'd taken a leave of absence at work. Sam couldn't be with them during this time. I expressed to Hilda that I wanted time to bond with the children. She completely understood. A bitch hated giving up all the potential commission but family came first.

Today, I was running a few errands and decided to stop at the nail salon for a pedicure. It didn't matter to me one bit that the kids were with me. Samantha was asleep in the car seat and Solomon was asleep across my lap. I lay back in the electronic chair, allowing it to massage me until I nearly fell asleep. Unfortunately, my ringing phone not only startled me but interrupted the relaxing time I was enjoying. "Hello."

"Hey girl." It was Gucci. "Did you hear about what happened?" Her mouth was still messed up. Therefore, it was difficult to understand what she was saying.

"Gucci, Pete said you shouldn't be talking until your jaw heals." I reminded her, pulling Solomon back who was sliding down my thigh. He was sleeping so good, he was drooling all over me.

"Fuck what Pete said!" She snapped. "Cartier done fucked around and got us into some shit!"

"I know. He was wrong for attempting to shoot up Mario's house. What if the baby had been hurt?" People did dumb shit for the sake of retaliation. They never stopped to think of the consequences of what could occur as a result of their actions. "And you know he shot up the wrong house don't you?" I wasn't the one to gossip but she needed to know the facts. "He shot up the neighbors' house. That seventy something lady was asleep in her bed; minding her business!" Sam had given me the scoop.

"What!?" She gasped.

"That shit has been all over the news. They were soliciting businesses in or around the community to assist the homeowners with repairing damages to both the exterior and interior that were a result of AK-47 bullets." The nail tech was filing my pinky toe too hard. Moving the phone away from my mouth, I gave her a piece of my mind, then rejoined the conversation with Gucci. "Mario said he would foot the bill for the damages because he felt bad."

"Man, I can't believe..." Gucci's sentence was left unheard. From my seat, I witnessed two chicks enter the nail salon. One of them was Tynika.

"Let me call you back." I didn't even wait for a response before I disconnected the call. Sliding the phone into my pocket, I picked up Solomon, and headed over to his mother. "You can't answer the phone, you can't check on your child, but you can come and get your nails done?" I had a straight attitude.

"He was with his father. He's cool." She dismissed the issue like it was nothing. Had the boy not been in my arms, it would've been on.

"What kind of mother are you Tynika? He's a one year old baby! You're ok with just dropping him off and never looking back?"

"Mina, I ain't got time for no lectures." She smacked her lips. "Since he's a problem, give him back, and I'll take him."

"Bitch, the only way you're going to get him

back is through court." I held onto Solomon for dear life. "He's not a problem! You're the problem!" I snapped. These young girls kill me having babies and treating them like a fashion accessory. "Solomon is not a purse or a pair of shoes. You can't just pick him up and put him down when you get ready." I was on the verge of tears only because I'd lost a child and here she was unappreciative of the blessing God bestowed upon her.

"Fine! Keep him. He was cramping my style anyway."

Chapter Fifty-Two
Nikki

The night Mrs. Crooks' house was shot up, Mario informed me the hit was meant for him. He explained everything then instructed me to head over to Anjela's house, she was expecting me. He had already dropped Junior off. Mario had tried to catch me on the phone before I left the airport but my phone was dead. Needless to say, I packed an overnight bag and got the fuck out of dodge.

"This shit is crazy!" Anjela was in the kitchen reading the newspaper. Junior was asleep on the couch next to me.

"What?"

"The beef Mario is involved in is making headlines." She rolled the newspaper up and tossed it at me. Sure as shit, on the front page of the paper was an article about the H.O.F. organization. The media reported the incident as a drug war. They also estimated the number of casualties to be somewhere around ten. The article went on to say that the Mayor didn't take kindly to thugs destroying his city. He was working with the city police to regain control of the situation and bring the responsible parties to justice. On the bottom of the article, there was a picture of the author. He was the same man who approached us when I brought Mario home from the hospital.

I laid the paper down across my stomach. I felt nauseous. This was bound to get much worse, real soon. Not only was Mario's life in jeopardy, his freedom was too. "I'm done with this shit! I stood from the couch. "It's always something."

"What's going on out here?" Carter stepped into the living room fully dressed with briefcase in hand. He placed the briefcase down on the table to adjust his tie.

"Girl stuff." Anjela kissed him on the cheek then handed him a titanium cup filled with coffee. She was loyal to me and hadn't ratted Mario out. Furthermore, it was none of his fucking business.

"Well you ladies have a great day and be safe. Things are getting crazy. Have you two seen the news?" He sipped from the cup. When he wasn't looking, I rolled my eyes. There was more to him than he was letting on.

"Yeah, we've seen the news. Have a good day." Anjela ushered him out the front door. Once he was gone, she looked at me. I was watching her with my lips twisted. "What?"

"Something ain't right with your man. That nigga is up to something."

"Up to what Nikki?" She blew out an audible

breath.

"Let's find out." I walked over to the briefcase but she stopped me before I could even touch it.

"Don't go in his stuff!"

"Girl bye!" I shrugged her off then returned to the metal contraption. It was some high-end, top of the line type shit with a finger scanner.

"Put it down!" She popped my hand and not a moment too soon. The front door opened and there appeared Carter.

"I would've knocked but the door was still unlocked," he proclaimed. "I forgot my briefcase."

"Nikki just noticed it. As a matter of fact, we were about to call you." She grabbed the heavy object from the table and handed it to him.

This time, I locked the door after he left. "We need to find out what his deal is."

"I don't need to find out a damn thing. All my shit is on the up and up and yours is too." She took a seat on the loveseat."

"But what about Mario?"

"Fuck him!" She snapped. "You need to stop being so concerned with him. One minute you're ready to go, then the next you want to be a ride or die bitch. Damn, pick a side and stay there!"

"You're right!" I nodded. "But I know it's no coincidence that both Carter and Cartier showed up outta nowhere." After the first time I met Carter, I'd informed Anj that his brother was Gucci's boyfriend. She didn't seem bothered one bit and decided not to tell him that she knew.

"My man said he had no idea what happened to his twin brother and I believe him. I mean who would lie about that?"

"Anjela, put that Harvard education to use!" I stomped my foot. "Your boy is a fucking fed. He could find Santa Clause if he really wanted to."

"Whatever girl! It's time for me to do some work. I'll be in my office if you need me." She waltzed down the hall. I was about to call Mario but my phone buzzed. It was a text from Maine asking if he could see me. After quick consideration, I texted back Anj's address.

Chapter Fifty-Three
Gucci

"What it do Eddie. It's time to collect." I stepped into the small barbershop in Highland Park with a nina on my side. Other than two other barbers, a lady, and two children, the place was just about empty. One child stood at the vending machine checking the slot for loose change. The other boy was in the chair with his eyes closed tightly.

"Give me two seconds and I got you." He brushed the small child's head to remove the excess hair then wiped him down with alcohol. After Eddie sprayed the little boy's head with oil sheen, he jumped down and ran over to his mother. The heavyset woman reached into her bra, handing her son a twenty. He ran back over to Eddie then placed the money in his palm. Eddie slapped him a low five then told him goodbye.

Once all the customers were gone, Eddie removed his smock. "It's in the back. You coming?" He gestured for me to follow him but I didn't move.

"You go ahead. I'll be out front." Although my team was right outside, I didn't know Eddie that well to be in close quarters with. He had only been on my list of distributors for a month. I had to get to know him before I felt more comfortable.

"No problem. I'll be right back." His raspy voice reminded me of Fred Sanford.

When I stepped outside, the crew was posted up and down the street. I felt like Obama or somebody with all the protection. "Yo, who the fuck is that?" My little homey Mondo pointed toward the red Nissan speeding down the block. Without delay, all my nigga's reached for guns, which were concealed underneath their shirts. My shit was also clutched tightly. Today was payday and everybody was on edge. Cartier wanted me to stay home because I wasn't really in a position to be out and about yet. However, I refused! I never missed the opportunity to collect money.

When the car approached us, it slowed down slightly but soon bypassed us like nothing was up. The minute everyone relaxed, we heard a commotion from inside the shop. POP! POP! BOOM! The gunfire seemed to come from everywhere. From my vantage point, I watched mirrors break and blood splatter. These niggas had attacked us from the back, using the red car as a distraction. "Fuck!" I heard Mondo scream. He'd been hit in the arm but it didn't stop him from shooting back. POW! POW! I watched two men wearing bandanas drop. A third bandana-wearing man was carrying the duffle bag I was there to collect. Not one to lose money, I aimed my pistol, letting loose several shots. "Fuck!" I had missed. The thief ducked and dodged several more bullets until he was able to escape through the backdoor. I wanted badly to run after him and reclaim my shit. However, the sirens told me to take it as a lost and get the hell away from here.

INDIA

Chapter Fifty-Four
Lovely

As Do It and Shawnie approached us, I saw his expression change from casual, to shock, then betrayal. Shawnie hadn't even paid any attention to me. If she had, the operation would've been blown. I tried not to make eye contact but it was hard. For weeks, I didn't believe I would see my family again. Now that they were a few yards away from me, I was conflicted. On one hand, I wanted to jump up from the table and run toward them. Then again, I didn't want to piss Santiago off. "I bought a bottle of *Ace of Spades* for your special day. It's my understanding that it's a very popular drink amongst the wealthy in America." He pulled the metallic gold champagne bottle from the black box and sat it on the table. "Almost five hundred dollars for one bottle is ridiculous." He stated as he chuckled. I wanted to remind him that his cigar hobby wasn't cheap. Instead, I smiled.

"Thank you, you didn't have to do that though. I won't be having a drink tonight."

"Why not?" He looked offended. "It's your birthday. I thought you wanted to celebrate."

"I do want to celebrate but after your brother spiked my drink, I won't ever be drinking again." I looked into his eyes, hoping he would understand I wasn't being ungrateful or disrespectful. I simply had a new respect for being sober.

"Ok fine." He placed the bottle back into the box. Rising from the table, he stated, "I'll go to the car and get your gift instead."

"What gift? You already bought me what I'm wearing."

"Well you didn't have any clothes," he smiled. "Your real gift is in the car. I'll be right back."

The second his back was turned, Do It told Shawnie to run along and made his way over to me. "What the fuck is up Lo? I thought you was fucking dead!" He was furious.

"I was drugged and kidnapped by some Mexican brothers, Santiago and Mauricio... They've been holding me hostage in their prostitution house a few miles from here." I tried to cram all of my words together for the sake of time. The car was a little ways away but Santiago ran fast.

"Let's go!" Do It urged.

"No." I shook my head. "He's with the mafia. If I get up and we're caught, he will kill us. Please leave and get Shawnie out of here."

"What about you?" He looked conflicted. "Fuck the mafia! I can't just leave you here."

"Do It, me and you ain't big enough to battle the Mafia, especially not on their turf and in their country. I'll be fine. Just go!"

My brother looked as if he wanted to say something else before he walked away. I sat there with a tear in the corner of my eye. *Had I just made a big mistake by letting my only opportunity slip away?* "Who was that and why was he talking to you?" Santiago took his seat at the table. The tenderness he left with was gone. He sat before me now wearing a scowl and breathing hard.

"Oh," I was trying to think fast. "He explained to me that his daughter was collecting shells and asked could he have the big one by my foot." I bent down and picked up the large seashell shaped like a horn.

"What did you say?"

"I told him no, obviously." I giggled. "This is our first date; I wanted to keep the seashell as a souvenir." Laying it on thick, he devoured every ounce of it.

INDIA

Chapter Fifty-Five
Nikki

Maine stepped into Anjela's condo smelling good and looking even better. The ash grey custom suit was tailor made and his loafers were Italian. The man exuded class every time I saw him. "What's up sexy?" He winked.

"Nothing much. What's up with you?" I blushed, closing the door.

"I just left a meeting, nothing major." As he scanned the living room, he noticed my son. He walked over and sat beside him. "What's up little man? I like your cars."

"Thank you." Junior continued to play with his toys.

"I have one of these. Maybe I can show it to you one day." He pointed to a motorcycle. "Would you like that?"

"Yes." Junior smiled. Maine patted his head then turned back toward me.

"So what brings you by?" I asked, still standing.

"Two things," he sighed. "The first reason is I wanted to see you. Secondly, I'm leaving for Mexico tonight."

"What?" I frowned. "So you're going back to

her?" I knew things were too good to be true.

"My ex got into some trouble. Her family called me for help." He stood. "Baby, it's not what you think it is." He tried to kiss me but I moved away out of respect for my son.

"Whatever!"

"Really, it's not like you should care anyway. You're still laying up with your ex-husband remember." He backed away from me.

"You came into my world, turned it upside down, and now you're leaving." I couldn't believe how gullible I was.

"Nikki, I swear I'll come back!"

"No you won't Maine, so just cut the bullshit! I was just someone you used to kill time with while you and that bitch sorted things out."

"Baby, come here." He pulled me close. "I'm only going to help a friend. But if you give me a reason to stay, I won't get on that plane." The look in his eyes was sincere. *Knock! Knock!* The sound of the door captured my attention. I pushed away from Maine then went to check the peephole. Right then and there I wanted to faint. Standing on the other side of the door was Mario.

"Oh shit!" I grabbed my stomach.

"What's wrong?" Maine came to my aid. I couldn't even speak. He got the hint then checked the peephole as well.

Knock! Knock! This time the knock was harder, louder, and raised the hair on the back of my neck. "Why aren't you answering the door? It's Mario. Security called, I told him to let him through." Anjela stepped into the living room and stopped dead in her tracks. "Oh shit!" She looked from Maine to me.

"I'm not about to hide behind this door like a bitch." Maine walked pass me, taking the liberty of letting Mario in.

"What took so lo..." He stopped midway through the sentence. "Nigga, whatchu doing here?" Gritting his teeth he sized Maine up.

"You need to be addressing your girl." Maine tossed me under the bus.

"Mario, I've been meaning to talk to you about something. Now is as good a time as any." I motioned for Anj to remove Junior from the room. She looked at me as if she hated to miss the drama.

"You fuckin' this mutha fucka?" The ferocious tone in Mario's voice made me jump.

"Mario calm down please."

"Look Nikki, I'm gonna give you and him privacy to talk. Call me later. My flight is scheduled to leave at nine." Maine kissed my forehead then left.

"Were you leaving with him?" Mario looked devastated.

"No!" I shook my head. "Baby, please calm down."

"Nikkita, I expected some foul shit from Gucci but not you." He spoke as if the wind had been knocked out of him.

"Rio, it's not like that."

"Well tell me why I come over here to see you, and you're entertaining your baby's daddy!?" He took a seat on the sofa.

"Maine came back in town awhile ago. Yes, we've spent some time together but..."

"You love him?"

"I love you Rio but I can no longer sit back and watch the streets take you from me. I've begged and I've begged you to leave the game. You keep brushing me off and I'm tired. I want to grow old with you but you're making it impossible. As much as I hate to say it, it's me or the streets." I held my breath. Mario sat silent for a second then stood. He walked over to me and tongued me down. Without a word, he pulled his lips away from mine then walked right out of Anjela's door. I was devastated. Once, again he had chosen the streets over me. As I broke down crying, Anjela stepped from the room with Junior by her side. Her mouth was wide open.

"Cuz, are you okay?"

"Just give me a few minutes. I'll be alright." I sniffed. BUZZ. BUZZ. My phone slid across the sofa. It was a message from Mario: The streets don't mean shit if I ain't got you. Grab your shit and let's get our family outta here!

INDIA

Chapter Fifty-Six
Mina

I couldn't believe Tynika's trifling ass had the nerve to give her son up without a second thought. Solomon was such a wonderful child. He deserved so much better. "Hello." Sam spoke into the phone. He was probably in a bad area because there was a little static in the background.

"You won't believe this shit." I was sitting in the car at the parking lot of the nail salon. Resisting the urge to sucker punch that bitch wasn't easy. Therefore, I packed up the kids and left without finishing my pedicure.

"What happened?"

"I finally ran into your baby's mother. I checked her about being at the nail salon but not having time to check on her son."

"What did she say?" Sam was all ears.

"Basically, she told me she didn't want him." I paused. "Her exact words were, "he's cramping my style anyway."

"What type of monkey shit is that!" Sam was upset.

"I know." I shook my head as if he could see me. "I was outdone!"

"I'm about to come over there and talk with

that hoe. What's the address?"

"Baby, there is no need to come up here. If she doesn't want him, it's her loss and our gain." I looked through the rearview. Both of the kids were silent but awake. "First thing next Monday morning you need to contact the court for full custody." Legally, I wanted the shit on record. "Tynika should not have the opportunity or the right to simply have a change of heart. Then decide she wants to be a mother again when it's convenient for her to do so."

"Mina we just brought home one child. Do you really think we can handle two?"

"Sam, that's not even a question! He didn't ask to be brought into this world! It's not his fault his mammy is a deadbeat!"

"You're right."

"Between the two of us, these children will be loved, spoiled, and raised the right way." I started the car.

"See Mina, that's why I love you. I've never had someone like you in my life. You always see the positive in every situation and you prove daily how down you are for a nigga."

"One day, I'm going to be your wife; it's a role I plan to take seriously. I love you and I'll always be here no matter what obstacles come our way."

"Mina the bible says a man that finds a wife, finds a good thing..." He paused. "I don't want to let my good thing get away from me."

"I'm not going anywhere." I pulled out into traffic and proceeded back to the hotel.

"Just to be sure, let's get married next week." His words brought tears to my eyes.

INDIA

Chapter Fifty-Seven
Gucci

After the shooting at the barbershop, Cartier put me on house arrest. Within twenty-four hours I was tired of house-sitting. I decided to take Maria out for ice cream. On the way out, I grabbed the mail, and flipped through the stack. There were a bunch of bills with my name on them. "What the hell?" I opened the first one. It was from the mortgage company. The second was from the car company and the third one was a credit card statement. Everything Cartier had purchased for me was in my name. Perplexed, I pulled out my cell phone on the way out and called him–his voicemail came on. *How in the hell did he get my social security number and why would he put shit he purchased with drug money in my name?*

About ten minutes later, I pulled into a parking space near the door of Cold Stone Creamery and called Cartier again–still no answer. Disconcerted, I needed an explanation. I slammed the phone down on the passenger seat then got out to retrieve Maria. That's when I noticed Cartier and that chick Anjela leaving the Chinese restaurant next door. They were holding hands and laughing like old friends. I slammed my car door then ran over to the happy couple. "What the fuck is this nigga? You two-timing me with her?"

"I beg your pardon." Anjela placed a hand to her chest. "My man wouldn't touch your ghetto ass with a ten foot pole."

"Bitch! That's not your man. He's my man! You better tell her Cartier."

"His name is Carter." She pointed to the dude with the suit and tie on.

"Look, there's obviously some big misunderstanding here," he smiled. It was then that I realized that although he looked like Cartier, he was slightly taller and little more toned. "My name is Carter Jones." He extended his hand.

"My man is a federal agent not some hoodlum like yours." Anjela's revelation was startling.

"Well uh." Carter pulled nervously on his tie.

"Tell her baby." Anjela provoked him but the man said nothing. "His twin brother is your man. They were separated as kids."

Something didn't feel right; I began to back away. Running to the car, I hopped in and put that bitch in gear. Fear enveloped my heart as I dialed Cartier one last time. "Hello."

"You bastard! You set me up!"

"What?" He played dumb.

"Your brother is fed! The gig is up." While

driving back home, I began to put two and two together. When Cartier turned himself in all those years ago, he was facing life. When I asked how he got out so early, he said it was because some evidence came up missing. In reality, Cartier had been released from prison with the help of his brother but not without a price. The H.O.F. organization had been on the FBI's radar for years. Fortunately, they could never build a case against us. I'd been in the streets long enough to know that Cartier cut a deal with Carter to set us up in exchange for freedom. "You put all those expensive items in my name to build a case against me you bastard."

"That's the game Gucci." He didn't even sound remorseful. "I told you loyalty ain't shit but a seven letter word."

"Rot in hell you bastard!" I hung up the phone and pulled onto my street.

By now, the place was swarming with feds. Carter realized the case was blown and had probably called every cop in the area to search for me. I reversed down the block like a bat out of hell. There was no way I would turn myself in. I looked in the backseat at Maria and broke down crying. I didn't know what to do or where to go. I had less than one thousand dollars on my person. For the first time in a long time, I was scared.

Chapter Fifty-Eight
Nikki

I left Anjela's condo that day with Junior on one hip and my overnight bag on the other. Mario promised he was done with the game. On the ride home, I tried to apologize for how I had been sneaking around with Maine. Mario said it was done and we would never speak of it again. I was elated he had forgiven me. I guess there's something to the saying "Love Conquers All." Anyway, the minute we hit the front door, he grabbed a hat and tossed destination ideas into it. Whichever one we picked was where we were headed. Amongst the list was Rio de Janeiro, Tahiti, and Paris. Either one of those would've been swell but Paris was what Junior picked out. That night, I booked our first class tickets and could barely contain myself. Just the thought of finally leaving Detroit had me antsy. I couldn't wait to start life anew. Little did I know what lay in store.

They say joy was supposed to come in the morning. However, on this particular morning, I was awakened by Mrs. Crooks' dog. He was barking up a storm. Therefore, I was unable to go back to sleep. Getting up from the bed, I walked across the hall toward the fourth bedroom. If he kept it up, that dog was gonna wake up the neighborhood. I lifted the blind to see what was going on. That's when I spotted the taskforce van parked in the alley. This wasn't a good sign. Fearing the worst, I ran back across the hall and tried to wake Rio. "Nik, let me sleep. The flight ain't 'til noon," he moaned.

"Get up. The police are downstairs about to kick the door in." I was petrified and Mario hadn't heard anything I said. "Get up!" I slapped his face, jolting him awake.

"What the fuck you hit me for?"

"The police are about to kick the door in." I spoke calmly although I was anything but calm.

"What?" He was now out of bed and on his feet.

"Go look out the back window. The van is parked in the alley," I pointed.

"Ain't no time for that. Just go in the room with Junior." He headed down the stairs.

"Where are you going?" I whispered.

"Ain't no sense in letting them tear the door off the hinges. I'ma open it and wait for them on the porch."

"Rio, I'm scared!" No matter how many times this had happened over the years, I was never prepared for it.

"No need to be scared, you know how this shit gon' play out. Just don't let my son see them take me away in handcuffs." He headed down the stairs and opened the front door. I knew my instructions were to go in the room with Junior. On the contrary, I had to make sure Mario was going to be okay.

Inching my way down the steps, I could hear the walkie talkies on the side of the house. "The suspect is on the front porch. I repeat, the suspect is on the front porch."

I made my way toward the front door just in time to see Mario lay down with both hands behind his back. He had on a pair of Nike basketball shorts and a wife beater.

"Can I at least give him a shirt and some shoes?" I ran outside as they read him his rights.

"Mrs. Wallace, my name is Daniel Townsend. I'm with the Federal Bureau of Investigations. You're under arrest with your husband for the RICO Act." Forcefully, he grabbed me and placed cuffs on my wrists.

"What!?" I couldn't believe this shit.

"We can talk down at the station." He pulled me off the porch in my nightgown toward one of the waiting squad cars.

"Don't say nothing Nik!" Mario yelled before getting into the back of a police vehicle.

"Officer, my son is in the house sleeping. Can I please call his grandmother?" My heart pounded. I had watched Mario be arrested numerous times. However, never had I gone to jail with him.

"What's the number?" He looked annoyed. I gave him Ms. Claudia's number, praying like hell she answered.

"Hello." She was sleeping.

"Ms. C, it's me. Mario and I are being arrested. Please come over to the house and get Junior now."

"Oh no Nikki!" She was obviously upset. "Baby, I'm on my way right now!"

"Call Mario's attorney..." I attempted to say before the officer ended the call.

"Let's go." He escorted me in the direction of the car. My heart stopped when I heard my son screaming from the porch.

"Mommy!" He cried hysterically. A female officer in a blue coat with yellow letters tried to console him.

"Junior, Granny is on the way. Mommy will be right back, I promise." My voice was strong and believable. Conversely, I felt helpless. By now, all of my neighbors were in the window or on their porches looking and whispering. The whole scene was like something out of a movie.

Once downtown at the FBI office, I was placed

in a small conference room and given a blanket. Then I was left alone for over an hour. My nerves were all over the place; I was jittery. I hadn't done anything to be arrested. Sometimes, we were simply guilty by association. "Mrs. Wallace, my name is Perri Kensington." A blonde female with blue eyes stepped into the room. I wasn't fooled one bit by the fake smile. This was part of the game.

"I want a lawyer." There was no need in going any further. Once I dropped the L word, there was nothing she could do.

"I can call one for you but that won't be necessary." She sat down across from me at the table. "Mrs. Wallace, I want to apologize on behalf of the FBI for arresting you in error. We're actually looking for Gucci Wallace, Mario's current wife."

"Am I free to go then?"

"Yes you are. I've arranged for an agent to take you home. Do you mind answering a few questions first?"

"I can't help you." I stood from the seat and headed for the door.

"Do you know where we can find Gucci?" She was only asking to see if the ex-wife would turn on the current wife. Her case files probably documented our disdain for one another. Even so, she was barking up the wrong tree. I was no snitch.

No matter how much I disliked Gucci, I wasn't going to make finding her easy.

Chapter Fifty-Nine
Lovely

The remainder of my date with Santiago went smoothly that evening. He was a perfect gentleman. The beachside dinner was awesome. We even went dancing afterwards. I learned a lot about him, such as how he and Mauricio ended up in the prostitution business. "We were born and raised in Mexico City, Mexico. Our family consisted of my mother, my brother, my grandmother, and me. We were poor, very poor." The blank stare into the distance revealed he was replaying childhood memories in his mind. "When I was about fourteen, I began working for Conseco Alverez, a known kingpin with the cartel. As a kid, my duties were never anything serious but I was with him all the time. I learned that he liked women, a variety of women," he smirked. "Mr. Alverez didn't care who they were or where they came from. He would rent rooms for hours just to have sex with everyone except his wife. As time went on, I noticed this was the way most of the cartel men operated. The only downside was some of the females became attached, or started running their mouths around town. No matter how much a man like Mr. Alverez cheated on his wife, he loved her. Therefore, he would kill someone dead before they had the chance to inform her of his infidelities. Needless to say, a lot of bodies turned up for that reason. It was a mess. But I had a solution." He looked at me. "I decided to save enough money to buy a house, my first house, and turn it into a place the cartel could come and relax. They wouldn't have to worry about their secrets and fetishes being exposed because my girls never left the premises. I left it up to my brother to acquire the women. Before we knew it, business was thriving."

"Wow! That's something to be proud of." I was being sarcastic.

"Come on, it's no different than selling drugs and murdering people." He used the terms to strike a chord that I wasn't perfect. There were demons in my closet as well.

"I did what I had to do for my family."

"And I did what I had to do for mine!" His voice elevated. "Look, let's not ruin your birthday with this nonsense." He held the door to the car open then we headed home. Overall, the date was nice and I did have fun. Santiago was different but I liked him. I earnestly wished we would have met under different circumstances.

For days following the date, my thoughts often traveled to seeing Do It. I partly expected him to bust down the doors at any moment. If I knew him, he had more than likely called Maine and tried to devise a plan. In all probability, Maine didn't care one bit what happened to me. Without Maine, Do It didn't stand a chance. "What are you doing down here?" Lucy asked when I approached the kitchen. She was standing at the sink looking out the window.

"I came to get something to drink. Is that okay?" Opening the refrigerator, I glanced over my choices of milk, water, orange or apple juice, and pop.

"There is a party in the front. You need to get whatever you're looking for and make your way upstairs." Her eyes never left the window. Casually, I grabbed some orange juice then walked over to see what she was looking at. My stomach turned when I saw a girl being held down and branded with the electric brander. She was fighting and screaming just as I had. I turned away from the window. The image had me sick to my stomach.

I grabbed a cup, poured my drink, and headed back up to my room. However, rather than taking the servant's hallway, I chose to bypass the parlor where the guests were and go up the main staircase. I could hear soft music and laughter. Easing the parlor door open slightly, I sneaked a peak. The smell of smoke filled my nostrils. "What are you doing?" Mauricio approached me.

"I was looking for Santiago," I lied.

"He's busy." Mauricio attempted to close the door in my face but I wasn't having it. I forced the door back open, scanning the room for Santiago. For some reason, thoughts of him and a whore crept into my head. I was slightly jealous.

"Encantadora what's wrong?" Santiago was not in the parlor. He was actually coming from the study with a black man. The familiar face hadn't changed one bit. In reality, having not seen it in so long actually made it look better.

"I had something to tell you but it can wait." I nervously dropped my glass.

"Let me get that for you Ms." The familiar face kneeled down to retrieve my glass. He was wearing a Tom Ford exclusive and smoking a *Gurka, His Majesty's Reserve.*

"Honey this is Maine, and Maine this is Encantadora, my future wife." Santiago introduced us. I could've died right there on the spot. I could tell Maine was bothered by my new title but didn't let on.

"Doesn't that mean Lovely in English?" He asked Santiago, never removing his eyes from me.

"Actually it does." I extended my hand; he

kissed it. Santiago frowned.

"We're in the middle of doing business. Go back to the room; I'll send for you later, " he interjected.

"Actually, I think I found what I'm looking for." Maine turned to Santiago. "How much for her?"

Santiago was taken aback. "She's not for sale my friend." He laughed nervously. "Come into the parlor. I'll show you my line-up."

"I want her." Maine hit him with a stone cold stare. "How much?"

"I said she's not for sale! You can choose someone else or you can be escorted out." Santiago opened the parlor door, beckoning for two security guards.

"I don't like my options," Maine retorted. "How about I take the girl and let you live?"

"Let me live? Are you insane? It's only one of you and fifteen of us, not to mention the members of the cartel." Santiago was beet red in the face.

"Suit yourself." Maine pulled a silver gun attached to a silencer from the waist of his pants then sent four bullets into Santiago's body. I watched in slow motion as his body flew backward into the security guards. I had no idea how Maine planned to get us out of this, but I prayed like hell it worked.

Chapter Sixty
Gucci

I'd been on the run for nearly two days. Maria and I had only managed to get to Lima, Ohio. It was only two hours away from Michigan but it was the best I could do. While we were on the road, two of my tires blew, and I had to get towed to the nearest town. The local mechanic was working on it and said it would be done today. I still didn't have a destination in mind. Even so, we had to keep it moving. With the tire situation, my funds had taken a hit. But there was still eight hundred dollars left.

I sat up on the bed in the motel and rubbed my head. The severity of my situation was weighing heavily on my mind. BUZZ. BUZZ. The phone vibrated. I checked the screen to see a private number. I knew it was the feds trying to track my whereabouts so I didn't answer. Then the motel phone rang. The sound frightened me so badly that I held onto my heart to keep it from leaping from my chest. Initially, I wasn't going to answer it. Then I remembered I told the mechanic I was staying here and to notify me when the car was ready.

"Hello."

"Gucci." The voice belonged to Bayani; I

cringed. "I told you once that your life depends on your word," he paused. "Now that we know your word doesn't mean shit, I guess your life doesn't either."

"Bayani, I had no idea what Cartier was up to." Until now, I had completely forgotten about the Filipino mafia.

"That's not my problem. You vouched for him, now you owe me." His voice was cold.

"I'm on the run myself. I don't have anything to give you at the moment." I stood and instinctively walked over to the blinds. There were several cars in the parking lot of the cheap motel. However, the only one that appeared to be out of place was the white Lexus. I could barely see the driver behind the tinted windows. Eerily, his lips moved in conjunction to the words Bayani was speaking into the phone. It had to be him.

"You will pay me in blood!" He hung up; my stomach rumbled. With him in the parking lot, at any moment, he could've kicked in the door. It was time to get out of here. Foremost, I had to think about my daughter. Thinking fast, I dialed the last person on earth I expected assistance from.

"Hello."

"Nikki, it's Gucci; don't hang up!" I paused. "I'm in trouble. I need your help."

"Are you okay? Where is Maria?" To my surprise she was actually concerned.

"We're okay but not for long." I walked over to the window and peeked through the blinds again. The Lexus was still there. "I'm at a place called the Wolfe Motel in Lima, Ohio. It's right off I-75."

"That's two hours away from here right?"

"Yeah, it is. I need you to come and get Maria for me. I can't keep going strong with her on my hip." I looked at my baby girl, blinking away the tears. It was going to kill me to part ways with her but it was in her best interest. As much as I hated to admit it, Nikki was my saving grace.

"Ok, I'm leaving as soon as I get Junior dressed." I could hear dresser drawers slamming.

"You might want to leave him with his father." Bringing him wasn't a good idea.

"Mario is in jail Gucci." Her words hit me all at once but I dared not ask questions on the phone. "I'll call you when I get there."

INDIA

Chapter Sixty-One
Mina

I couldn't believe it was my wedding day and no one was there to bare witness except Sam's children, the pastor, and his assistant. Gucci had gone AWOL and I had no other family. I looked at myself in the dresser mirror and smiled. For the first time in a long time, I was genuinely happy. Everything we'd been through lately had somehow made our relationship stronger. *Tap. Tap.* Sam opened the bedroom door. I ran into the closet to hide. "It's bad luck to see the bride before the wedding fool."

"I need to talk to you." His voice concerned me.

"What is it?" I stepped from behind the closet door to see my man standing there in a button down shirt and a pair of jeans. "Where are the kids?"

"The kids are in their rooms." He took a seat on the bed, patting the spot beside him.

"What is it Sam? You're scaring me!"

"Amina, I love you more than life. You've proven your love for me through and through. Many women would've given up on me after all I put you through. But you didn't; that means the world to me. You love my children and they love you. In my wildest imagination, never could I have dreamed I'd be blessed with such a wonderful woman. To be honest, I don't deserve you."

"What are talking about?" I lifted his chin which was buried in his chest.

"We vowed to have no more secrets but I've been keeping something from you."

"It better not be another child!" I stood.

"No. It's nothing like that." He stood with me.

"Well spit it out." I couldn't believe this boy and all his fucking secrets.

"This secret has been burning a whole in my heart and I wanted you to know before you said I do."

"Depending on what it is, I may not be saying I do." I backed away, folding my arms.

"Me and Gucci messed around a few times but it was nothing."

"What do you mean it was nothing!?" I screamed. He grabbed my arms to prevent me from swinging at him. "You fucked my friend?" Tears gathered in the corners of my eyes.

"Mina, baby I'm sorry. I was going through some shit."

"That's no excuse Sam!" I pushed him off of me. "I was calling her for relationship advice and you guys were screwing! Here I am standing by your side like a real bitch, and you're sneaking around with my friend!?" Wiping my face, I ruined my makeup. "I was thinking I wasn't good enough for you when in fact I'm too damn good for your whack ass!" I took my ring off then hurled it across the room. "Fuck you Sam! I'm done."

Chapter Sixty-Two
Nikki

It was a little after ten when I exited the freeway and called Gucci's motel room. She told me to pull around back and meet her at the backdoor of the shabby motel. When I pulled up, I saw her standing there with Maria in a car seat. I left the car idling while I ran inside. "Thank you so much for coming." She hugged me then handed the baby over.

"What are you going to do?" I felt bad for her. She looked as if she hadn't slept a wink in days. Her clothes were wrinkled and her hair was a mess.

"I'ma keep running until they find me I guess," she shrugged. "Was there a white Lexus parked out front?"

"Yes." I recall bypassing the vehicle on my way through the parking lot.

"Shit!" She cursed.

"Why? Who is that?"

"Cartier and I did a deal with him awhile back. He found out Cartier was a rat. Now he's gunning for me because I vouched for him." She shook her head.

"That shit has been all over the news. They've arrested twelve other people including Mario on drug trafficking for the H.O.F. organization. You and him are also being charged with the RICO Act." I'd come to learn that RICO stood for Racketeer Influenced and Corrupt Organizations. It's a United States federal law that pushes for extended criminal penalties and a civil cause of action for acts performed as part of an ongoing criminal organization. The RICO Act allows the *leaders* of a syndicate to be tried for crimes in which they ordered others to execute or assisted them with. "Gucci, they have pictures, receipts, and even you on tape during a meeting with the Pilipino." I wanted her to know what she was dealing with. "It's not looking too good."

"Nikki, I didn't mean to get Mario in trouble," she sighed. "Cartier set me up. He had me split up H.O.F., purchased that shit in my name, and put my life on the line with the Pilipino mafia."

"Gucci, your best bet might be to turn yourself in." At least being inside under police protection was safer than being out here all alone.

"Hell no! The mafia has connections everywhere. The minute I'm in custody, I'll be a sitting duck waiting for Bayani's people to kill me. My odds are better if I stay on the run."

"Suit yourself." I couldn't force her to do anything. She was a grown ass woman who had gotten herself into this mess. I'm sure she would figure out how to get out of it. "It's about to rain so we better get out of here."

"Bye Maria. I love you!" Gucci bent down to kiss her daughter. My heart ached for her. As a mother, I could only imagine what she was experiencing. I waved goodbye to Gucci who stood in the doorway. After strapping Maria in, I closed the door, and got into the driver's seat. I wanted to drive away but I couldn't leave her alone. I exited the car again then ran back up to the building. "I can't leave you here, come on!" By now, the rain was coming down hard.

"I can't put you in danger." She shook her head.

"Just get in the trunk. I'll drop you off at the Greyhound station." My heart would be more at peace knowing I got her to safety.

"Ok." She said after a few minutes of contemplation. She ran out into the rain and I lifted the trunk. She got in quickly then I closed the trunk behind her. Once again, I got into the driver's seat and pulled away from the motel. The white Lexus was still parked out front as I drove by.

The Greyhound station was a mere two miles away. I surveyed the area before letting her out. "Did anyone follow you?"

"No, it's all good." I reached into my purse then handed her two large stacks of money. When she called earlier, I hit the closet safe and withdrew it just in case. It was a total of five thousand dollars. Although the feds had raided my house, they couldn't take any of my property because Mario and I were legally divorced. His name wasn't on the deed. Furthermore, I had legit money from my book sales "Take this." I shoved it into her hand.

"Thank you Nikki!" She looked as if she wanted to cry.

"Now go ahead and get a ticket on the next thing smoking. When you reach a destination, grab a minute phone, and keep in touch."

"Thank you again!" She made a mad dash toward the bus station. I didn't know what was going to become of the situation but my prayers were with her. I hopped into the driver's seat then put the car in gear. It was time to get back home.

Being out in the rain in the middle of nowhere had a bitch on edge. To calm my nerves, I turned on Tamar Braxton's CD. Hearing her talk about "Love and War" gave me a lot to ponder. *Should I purchase another flight ticket, or should I stay in Michigan for Rio?* He needed me now more than ever. Either way, I was done being a hood wife and could actually use the time away from him to go my separate way. So many thoughts flooded my mind as I merged onto the highway. BEEP! BEEP! The horn on the car behind me was distracting. The driver must've been in a hurry. I sped up to allow him to pass. BEEP! BEEP! Now they were riding my bumper with the high beams on. I couldn't see shit. Therefore, I merged into the passing lane in an attempt to shake him. That's when I realized it was the same white Lexus from the motel. "Oh shit!" I mumbled. I didn't want to alarm the kids but I was scared. Speeding down the highway, I grabbed my phone then dialed 911.

"What's the emergency?" The operator asked.

"I'm being followed by an aggressive driver on I-75 North!" I switched back to the middle lane, the white car did the same. This time he bumped the back of my SUV. "Please help me; I have two children in the car and I'm pregnant!"

"What's your exact location on I-75 North ma'am? Can you see a mile marker?"

I was driving too fast to see any of that. "Please ma'am! Just use the GPS tracker on my cell phone!" I screamed. By now the children were both crying. POP! A shot was fired into my back tire causing my vehicle to sway from side to side. The shot might've slowed me down but I was not stopping. BOOM! Another shot entered the window shattering the glass.

"Please get us help now!" My car was now rolling on the rim, which meant it was about to stop. Sparks were flying everywhere. I maneuvered the whip as best I could. Except one final shot to the other back tire sent us spiraling out of control. Then, the driver of the other vehicle slammed his car into mine.

I went flying into a ditch at a speed of almost ninety miles per hour. CRASH! The SUV only stopped when it connected with a tree. My body was hurled through the windshield and catapulted on the hood amongst shards of glass. I couldn't move my body but at least I wasn't dead yet. I could hear three things distinctively. The first was the sound of footsteps coming in my direction. The second was the cries of the kids who sounded far away as if they had been tossed from the truck also. The last thing I heard was the 911 operator. I still had the phone in my hand. "Ma'am help is on the way!"

To be continued…

INDIA